# HELEN SLOANE'S DIARY

# HELEN SLOANE'S DIARY

Jeff Lucas

**Authentic**

MILTON KEYNES ● COLORADO SPRINGS ● HYDERABAD

Copyright © 2008 Jeff Lucas

14  13 12  11  10  09  08    7  6  5  4  3  2  1

First published 2008 by Spring Harvest Publishing Division and
Authentic Media

9 Holdom Avenue, Bletchley, Milton Keynes, Bucks, MK1 1QR, UK
1820 Jet Stream Drive, Colorado Springs, CO 80921, USA
OM Authentic Media, Medchal Road, Jeedimetla Village,
Secunderabad 500 055, A.P., India

www.authenticmedia.co.uk

Authentic Media is a division of IBS-STL U.K., limited by
guarantee, with its Registered Office at Kingstown Broadway,
Carlisle, Cumbria CA3 0HA.  Registered in England & Wales No.
1216232. Registered charity 270162

British Library Cataloguing in Publication Data
A catalogue record for this book is available
from the British Library

ISBN: 978-1-85078-797-6 (green cover)
ISBN: 978-1-85078-800-3 (pink cover)

Green Cover Design by David Lund
Pink Cover Design by Rachel Myatt
Print Management by Adare
Printed and bound in Great Britain
by CPI Bookmarque, Croydon, CR0 4TD

**Dedicated to Terry and Jayne**
Celebrating a new chapter in your lives . . .
With much love

## ACKNOWLEDGEMENTS

Writing as a 27-year-old woman is a new experience for me! This book would not have been possible without the talents of Tamsin Kendrick, who is a gifted writer and poet. She not only allowed me to peer into the mysterious space which is the twenty-something female Christian mind, but helped greatly with ideas, plot twists, character colour and words. And she came to Eastbourne and Colorado to help make this book happen. Eastbourne is lovely, but I think she preferred Colorado . . .

Thanks Tamsin.

As ever, I thank my faithful, blunt, kind, eagle-eyed editor, Ali Hull. Working with you is always a treat, Ali.

My thanks to my daughter, Kelly, my favourite social worker in the universe. Kelly is nothing like Helen, but shares the same profession: her insights were invaluable.

Chris and Jeanne, thanks for the beach house – the perfect place to finish a book . . . and thanks for our wonderful friendship.

And Kay, you smiled and were unfailingly kind and understanding during the mad writing time. You've been smiling in my direction for quite some time now. I love you for it.

Great. I've begun. Here goes.

I, Helen Sloane, have now joined the ranks of the thoughtful literati who keep a journal. In the pages that follow I shall chronicle (hopefully with wit and flair) the hopes, dreams, fears, successes and failures that unfold in the coming year. Who knows what stunning riches of wisdom might flow from my two-fingered typing as I reflect here upon my journey? Great trees grow out of tiny acorns . . .

Tonight I'm totally exhausted from my first day back at work after the Christmas hols, so the odds are against me writing anything that might win a Nobel Prize for Literature. Perhaps tomorrow.

Life as a newly qualified social worker (two months in the job, working on the Child Care Team) is demanding. The holiday break already seems like ancient history. Tonight my head's buzzing with client updates, court papers, chatter from the team strategy meeting and what seems like an entire filing cabinet of case notes.

Add to this my role as a house group leader in Frenton-on-Sea's New Wave Christian Fellowship (someone obviously thought that the 'new wave' maritime play on words was a bright idea), plus the demands of my busy social calendar and the result is a frantic life navigated at high speed. I hardly have time to breathe, never mind think, pray or reflect – hence this diary.

My mildly demented best friend Vanessa (mildly being the operative word) came up with the idea yesterday during our New Year's Day lunch together. Vanessa is either living on a different spiritual plane from me or needs medication. The problem is, I think you need to be a little mad to be as nice as she is. Maybe that's her secret. She goes to the big church in town, Infusion, which has a high energy worship team and an age demographic of about twelve. I have been tempted to go there myself but the band seem to be on Duracells and I don't think I could maintain that level of consistent ecstasy.

We were talking about where our lives were heading and sharing our goals for the New Year. She said that she was determined to see 'a clear impact in the heavenly realms, so that every blessing that has been preordained for me since the very beginning of time would be made fully manifest in a way that would cause demons to tremble and angels to dance.'

I said that I wanted to get fit and lose a stone. She rebuked me in the ever-so-sweet way that only she can and offered me the vital advice that our Lord Jesus never owned a treadmill and that John the Baptist, he who prepared the way of the Lord, didn't do Atkins. I was tempted to comment about all that low-carb snacking on locusts and wild honey, but couldn't be bothered. I was too busy day-dreaming about my real goal for this year . . . which I can't bring myself to write down just yet, but may in a moment . . .

Anyway, back to Vanessa as she rabbits on. I was of course listening intently and was in no way playing with my hair and wondering what I'd look like as a redhead . . .

'Spiritual growth comes from considered reflection, Helen. Saint Simeon Stylites sat on top of a pole for many years in complete solitude, covered in sores and his own filth. His only contact with the rest of the world was a bucket used for receiving food and disposing of his faeces. But I bet that man knew himself and knew his God.'

Decided that buckets and poles should not play any part in my spiritual life this year, but I knew I had to do something when Vanessa put her hand on my arm and asked, 'Helen, can you remember the last time that God clearly answered one of your prayers?'

I racked my brains for a second or two and had to confess that nothing immediately came to mind. Maybe I should pray for a better memory and then, when I get it, I'd remember to be grateful. It was then that Vanessa said she was convinced that a journal would help my amnesiac tendencies. Her advice was blunt. 'Make a commitment, Helen. Write stuff down every day.'

Her idea clicked with me immediately, because I've got a great feeling about this year and I don't want to miss a moment, plus a daily appointment with my laptop beats buckets and poles hands down.

Vanessa says that she's been praying a lot and announced that she feels that this will be the year of breakthrough, which sounds very nice. I have to be honest, though – call me Thomas if you like (the doubting disciple, not the Tank Engine), but I'm not sure about the way Vanessa gives each year a spiritual tag. We've been friends for ages, so over the last decade she's made a few predictions and I'm not convinced that they've been fulfilled. Last year was supposed to be the year of harvest and that the one before that was the year of an open heaven, which followed the year of refreshing. Maybe she's right, but all this sounds a bit Chinese to me (year of the rat and all that) and I can't honestly say that we've seen too much spiritual harvest or notable refreshing in Frenton-on-Sea. And the only open heaven we experienced two years ago was record rainfall in August. The deluge washed half the beach away and left piles of stinking seaweed, which I don't think was much of a blessing, unless you're into do-it-yourself seaweed spa wraps.

Vanessa also says that this year God is going to do something in Frenton that will 'reverberate around the nations and traumatise the very powers of hell'. I do love her, but it's unlikely that our rather grey little town with half a windswept pier is going to become the epicentre of God's purposes for planet Earth.

And yet I feel guilty for thinking that Vanessa is slightly off her head. When does asking questions about this stuff become cynicism? When does not asking questions become sheer stupidity? I can't help thinking that questions help us towards a more realistic, mature faith. So why does asking them make me feel so guilty?

Too tired to decide.

I suddenly realised that two of my very favourite people – Vanessa and my mother – are both quite odd when it comes to spiritual issues, but for totally different reasons.

I wondered if this is why I feel confused about faith for so much of the time.

One other thing: I am going to follow a 'Read through the entire Bible in one year' course, although because of the rush this morning I managed to read Genesis chapters 1-4 in 37 seconds. Perhaps I should do a 'Read through the entire Bible in 45 minutes even if you take a five minute coffee break' course instead. *And* I am going to get fit and thin (not waif-like à la Keira Knightley who probably only eats once a month) but just enough to enable me to be rescued from a blazing inferno by a gorgeous fireman without giving him a double hernia.

Well I think that's it for today. I am feeling rather happy to have completed my first diary entry. A good start.

I'm excited about the unswerving discipline that I'll employ to record my thoughts every day without fail, absolutely, I vow it solemnly to God, mark my words, so be it and Amen.

*Lord, here's my year. Stay close. Amen.*


## TUESDAY JANUARY 9th

**7.15pm**

Can't believe that a whole week has gone by and I completely forgot that I am now committed to keeping a journal. Note to self: must do better – not a great display of discipline – and obviously no answer to prayer yet about getting a better memory. Have decided to go on a 40 day fast, to create a slimmer, more godly me, as well as giving me a nifty detox. I did go to the gym today, which was awful and not only because of the excruciating torment inflicted by those evil weight-training machines that were probably in use during the Spanish Inquisition, alongside the rack. The pain came from the irritating presence of old Mrs Hemming from church (don't mean to be ageist here; we've got some totally wonderful elderly people in our church, but Mrs Hemming definitely isn't one of them). I don't think her problem has anything to do with age, though. She has probably been practising being unpleasant from a very early age and now has it down to a fine art.

She goes to the gym once each month to do her 2 miles per hour walk/crawl on the treadmill and, as she says to anyone who'll listen, she does it 'to be salt and light in the community and reach out to the lost'. She's certainly like salt, or at least the feeling of salt when it's rubbed into a wound. And as for being a light, she certainly stands out from the crowd, but that's because she's tortoise slow; it's like a watching a waxwork in a leotard. She always wears her fluorescent multi-coloured lycra all-in-one, an outfit that was probably highly fashionable when Noah was into floating zoos. Worst of all, she wouldn't shut up while I was sweating my way through my workout. She follows me around the gym, parks herself on the machine next to mine and blethers on. She must have muscles of iron – in her jaws.

Okay, feel a little guilty writing all this about Mrs Hemming, not only because we Christians are supposed to love absolutely everybody with the exception of the devil, but also because Mrs Hemming is married to Mr Hemming (am unaware that either one of them actually has a first name) and I don't like him either. He's the senior deacon in our church, which means that (a) he knows loads of the Bible and quotes it endlessly – usually out of context and (b) he's seen about eleven ministers come and go and, however good they are, Mr Hemming gives the impression that he's really the one in charge and so (c) even though he's painful and loud and rude, most people in the church are afraid of him and rarely challenge what he says and does. The only person he seems to be afraid of is his wife. Also, some of us live with a niggling worry that we do need to respect our leaders even if they're obnoxious, so we don't like to take him on. Vanessa is always banging on about making sure we bless and honour our leaders, whatever they're like. Another tricky one to think through . . .

Mrs Hemming could talk for England and today I felt like blessing her with a slap; I think she's such a gossip. She says she loves to 'share' and manages to whisper scandalous rumours about people under the guise that she is passing on prayer requests. 'We need to know what's happening, Helen dear', she hissed as I fought the urge to die during my fourth set of reps on the bench press, 'so that we can pray more faithfully and accurately.' She then told me about one of the deacons whose teenaged daughter apparently smoked dope at a New Year's Eve party.

'We need to pray that that wretched girl will see some sense and come to true, heartfelt repentance', she said. 'And also that God will give the diaconate wisdom to know if her father is still biblically qualified to serve in leadership, what with him having such a disgustingly wayward child . . . '

Totally disagree with her notion that someone is disqualified to lead because of the behaviour of their adult children and longed to shove her face into some of my case notes to see what the real world is like, but I needed all available oxygen for the challenging task of breathing. I just grunted, which I think she thought meant that I was agreeing.

I'm starving. 40 day fast starting to bite now. No pain, no gain. I'm pushing through.

**9pm**

I have decided to bring the 40 day fast to an end as I am nervous of anorexia, malnutrition and other issues that might lead to an untimely death. Besides, I'm in negative calorific balance due to all that wickedly demanding gym activity today, plus the nervous tension exerted listening to Mrs Hemming's time of sharing. Unfortunately I ordered in a Chinese take-away and followed it up with some of Ben &

Jerry's finest. For some odd reason, Mrs Hemming's grating-like-a-chainsaw monologue mildly depressed me and gave me a tinge of a hopeless 'What's the point in bothering with discipline if being spiritual might transform me into being a tiresome old bat?' feeling and, with my defences down, I went into calorific overdrive and my snacking was the equivalent of diving head first into a trough. Hope was slightly rekindled by the heavenly crispy duck.

Then Dad called to see how my work week was going. He worries that I'll struggle to deal with the emotional weight of my career choice. He's a quiet thoughtful type – the most fabulous listener I've ever met. Despite the fact that he's a man of few words, I'm certain about two things – he utterly worships my mother, even though they're so different – and his view of me is wonderfully close to adulation, which of course I like a lot. I told him about my 40 day fast that had turned into a 12 hour fast and he said that he was relieved to hear of my decision to end it because, as he said, 'Helen darling, with the warp speed of your life, you need nourishment.' Mind you, as a retiree who is now on Frenton-on-Sea Borough Council, he manages to live a high velocity life himself.

Then he put Mum on the phone and she agreed, but then she went on to tell me about her new aduki-bean mango bran diet, which sounded like a sure recipe for a gastric tropical storm.

Time for bed.

## WEDNESDAY JANUARY 10th

My Bible reading today was in Genesis 6, about the Flood. Reading the story again brought back memories of my school days, when we had a Christian youth worker visit our school and he did a question and answer session. Someone went on the attack and asked him why God did something so horrific as flood the earth. The poor lad looked completely lost and there was a very long silence. Finally he spluttered, 'I have no idea why God did that, but he did promise that he'd never ever do it again.' Smiled at the memory, but wondered again why God did that . . . Had lunch with Laura at a pizza place: lovely extra thick stuffed crust Canadian bacon and pineapple perhaps made slightly healthy by the bits of iceberg lettuce on top, followed by Banoffee Pie. And cream. And a chocolate mint and a latte to finish.

The main thing that happened today is that my house group from church didn't happen tonight, which I quite liked. I love the group and it's fairly easy co-leading it with my friend James, but when I found out that two or three of the group are either away or struggling with the sniffly cold thing that's going around (which Vanessa says we warriors of faith should be impervious to), we decided to cancel the evening and I stayed home and watched TV. Nice.

## FRIDAY JANUARY 12th

Once again I've missed another couple of days of journalling and defaulted on my Bible reading plan too. This discipline stuff isn't as easy as I thought. But I have had my first attempt at the Tropical Storm diet, which meant that most of the day was spent seated . . .

I had coffee with Vanessa after work tonight and told her about my lingering irritation/temptation towards inflicting grievous bodily harm on the grievous busybody that is Mrs Hemming. Vanessa said that Mrs Hemming isn't the problem, but that Satan is. Had a terrible thought – that sometimes Mrs Hemming and the Prince of Darkness share very similar behavioural patterns. Is Mrs Hemming actually Satan incarnate?

Vanessa suggested that I was going through a time of spiritual warfare. 'You must be doing something right, Helen', she insisted, presumably to cheer me up, but I decided that her notion that the advent of tough times implies that we're doing something good is odd, especially if you happen to live in Ethiopia, where every day is a battle whether you're doing something right or not. Wondered how many other old wives' tales we Christians trade about life unthinkingly. Didn't challenge Vanessa about the idea, but then perhaps that's how these notions spread – when we don't have the courage to confront them, they get passed on.

Vanessa is also reading a best-selling book from America about the Second Coming, which hasn't helped her sanity one bit. She's convinced that we're all now steering our way through the end-time apocalyptic battleground and that warfare in our lives is raging because of the strategic place of Frenton in God's eschatological masterplan. I struggle with the idea that Frenton plays a part in what Vanessa describes as the great conflict to come. Can't imagine fifty million crispy-duck munching Chinese troops showing up here to wrestle with the Great Russian Beast on our muddy beach . . .

Despite thinking, again, not out loud, that Vanessa is either very close to God, or very much in need of sedation, I *do* think she's right in some of the things she says. She does talk in riddles and can be unbearably spooky and does some very strange things because she believes that God is talking to her and yet, despite her oddness, she can be very wise. She said that I should be brutally honest in my journal . . .

. . . which brings me to my unmentioned secret furtive goal for this New Year . . . which is . . .

. . . to have sex. That's it, I've written it down and despite the rather unflattering flush of red-faced embarrassment that probably makes me look like a lobster as I tap away here, I *have* written it down, because it's true. I want to have sex, preferably while I am still young enough to experience it without dying during the process. To put it as bluntly as that perhaps makes me sound like Helen the scarlet woman/brazen hussy Sloane, fit only to hang out with Rahab the harlot, or even that Jezebel who was snacked on by dogs. So perhaps I need to clarify my urgent and indeed desperate declaration of my need for sex by saying that I *do* want sex as a married person, which means that, yes, of course, I want to hear wedding bells. But I need to own up to the fact that I frantically want to hit the sack as well as walk the aisle. And I would like God to know that I think I'll spontaneously combust if this doesn't happen soon. It's better to marry than burn, say the Scriptures, and right now a quick 999 call to bring out the fire brigade would be in order, not least because it would cause a few musclebound firemen to beat a pathway to my door. Whoops, I'm back to daydreaming about firemen again . . .

And I am getting rather fearful; there does seem to be a bit of a shortage of sensible men in the church, especially ones with less than three heads. So may this be the year. Hope so. Given the choice between being an eighty-year-old virgin and being ritually disembowelled, I think I'd cheerfully wave my lower intestines goodbye, especially after the experience of Mum's wonder diet. Have decided that to write something in this journal everyday is a little too demanding – but will try to do at least a couple of entries a week.

*Lord, you know me and love me with all my struggles. Help me to rest in you. Amen.*

## MONDAY JANUARY 15th

I had one of those lovely weekends where not much happened to write about but it was relaxing and nice. Unfortunately my alarm clock battery gave up the ghost Saturday night and I overslept, which meant I missed church. I felt guilty and pleased in almost equal measures. I love our church, but it was wonderful to have that extra couple of hours on Sunday morning to myself. I hoovered the flat and read the Sunday paper. It felt strangely decadent not being in church, sort of naughty and nice.

I got back to work today and hit the ground running. It was a mad day, including a particularly difficult initial home visit to a girl called Hayley, who makes Linda Blair in *The Exorcist* look like Little Bo Peep. Have decided to write in my journal about Hayley – I can't possibly journal here about every child that I meet, otherwise this diary is going to feel like a set of case notes and I'll run out of energy to write it. Suffice it to say that young Hayley is going to be a challenge.

She's sixteen and dresses like a stripper with a penchant for white, let loose in the children's section of H&M. White shoes, white pedal pushers, white top and a very obvious white G-string (with red diamanté spelling out *1% angel, 99% devil* underneath. The *1% angel* bit is probably an exaggeration. *100% adolescent nightmare* would be more accurate, but then that's a lot of diamanté and I don't think the G-string is big enough.

Poor girl. I had to suspend her parents' visiting rights over Christmas, as last time she saw them, they'd both ingested half a pub's worth of alcohol and had a fight. A fight that ended with her dad locking Hayley in the bathroom with a knife to her throat, threatening to do her in if her mother didn't break up with some guy called Kevin. It was three hours before the police managed to diffuse the situation. Talk about playing happy families . . .

About the only thing that Hayley said today was that, with my complexion, I couldn't carry off green, my favourite colour. Anyway, despite the fact that she obviously loathes me, I hope she managed to enjoy a normal Christmas for once, without all that madness around her. She's currently been staying with her aunt and uncle, who seem slightly better adjusted than her parents: slightly being the operative word. It's so unfair; some people just don't have a chance in life.

Nothing much else to report. Wrote a letter to Bruno, my brother, who is working on a cruise ship in the Caribbean. I try to send him a few lines every couple of months, although he rarely writes back.

Have now done enough writing for one day.

*Lord, help me with Hayley. And keep Bruno safe, wherever he is.*

## TUESDAY JANUARY 16th

Thank you. Thank you. Thank you. Yes, that would be me lavishing praises on my amazing, generous (and not to mention powerful and loving) Father, God that is, not my dad, although he is pretty stunning too. You'll never guess what happened to me on the way home! I bumped into Robert and Nola Marsh, otherwise known as our lovely pastor and his lovely wife and they told me that New Wave Christian Fellowship is employing a new member of staff. And we are not talking about any old member of staff – no! I'm not talking some dull-as-dishwater assistant minister or children's worker who thinks that multi-media is a presentation involving Fuzzy-felt. No, no, NO! We are talking about a real, in-the-flesh, young, enthusiastic, and most importantly MALE and SINGLE worship leader, fresh out of Bible college.

The conversation in the High Street basically involved me awkwardly coaxing details about him out of Robert and Nola, whilst at the same time trying not to sound like a desperate, single 27-year-old, which of course I am. Nola, by the way, was wearing a rather stunning blue skirt I saw in the sale at Monsoon last week but felt I was a little too rounded to fit into. I must stay off those triple chocolate cookies and perhaps embrace the way of bran muffins in accordance with Mother's advice and move to a figure more like Keira's. Anyway . . .

. . . our new worship leader is Kristian Vivian Rogers and he likes to use all three names. Apparently he was supposed to be introduced to the church a couple of weeks ago but God told him to go to the South of France or somewhere with some friends, so he's starting this weekend instead. YES! He's a worship leader *and* sensitive to the voice of the missionary God. I'm ecstatic. I might be in the single Christian girl's fifth heaven. Now all I need to do is quietly assassinate those annoyingly attractive worship band backing singers. I secretly call them the Muppets, because they always take off their shoes and jump around whilst smiling manically at the congregation. I'm sure all that removing of shoes must constitute some sort of health risk . . .

. . . I have just looked up the meaning of *Kristian* and apparently it means Christian, which, I suppose, is no great revelation. *Vivian* appears to be a girl's name . . . which is worrying . . .

Anyway, once I was on the computer checking the meanings of names, I figured that it couldn't do any harm to see if I could find a photo of him. It's not like I was stalking him or anything – in fact as a member and indeed a house group leader of New Wave Christian Fellowship, I feel that it is my right and duty to know as much as I can about members of our staff leadership team. I googled his Bible college and found a graduation picture of him and he is, wait for it, GOOD-LOOKING! And we are not talking *just* mildly good-looking, we are talking good-looking in a love stud, guitar-playing, floppy blond curtains hair and big baby blue eyes way. Alright, alright, I'm a stalker. But it was worth it. Just started to daydream about what might be in the future and then remembered the past and felt a tinge of depression . . .

Okay, Vanessa said I should be brutally honest in my journal. So . . .

I've never had much luck with Christian men. The last Christian guy I dated was at university, yes, that's the ancient history that was UNIVERSITY, about a million years ago. His name was Aaron and he dumped me because, as he was handing out leaflets about the CU at the student union nightclub one day, he happened to bump into me. Actually, he didn't bump into me so much as I happened to drunkenly fall off a table and land on his head. He wasn't terribly impressed and the next day he rang me up (early in the morning, deliberately I reckon, because he knew I'd have a thumping hangover) and told me he felt that 'we had different agendas'. Which basically meant he thought my agenda was to be a drunken Jezebel and his was to be so holy he would forgo death and be whisked to heaven in a flaming chariot or something.

It was stupid of me, I know, but I was a bit intoxicated with the feeling of freedom that slams into a lot of bright Christian young things when they head to Uni, hence my over-indulgence in tequila that night. It was just one night and the horrendous Lazarus-before-Jesus-came-by type experience that I had the next morning cured me of getting drunk for good – but he still dumped me because of it.

The ironic thing is (according to Vanessa, who found out from her cousin's best friend's brother) that, since finishing Uni, he's had some sort of existential crisis and has denounced God, quit his job as an Inland Revenue inspector and now scrawls Friedrich Nietzsche quotes all over his clothes. She said that her cousin's best friend's brother bumped into Aaron in a park and he was wandering around mumbling to himself. When asked what was wrong he started to cry and grabbed the guy's shoulders and said something like 'the poor birds, the poor birds, the white bread kills the birds, it expands in their stomachs and chokes them! It's killing them and they don't know it. And it's all because we wanted to make it uniform and all the same. They think that it's food, they're glad to receive it but it's a lie, a lie that will eventually break them.' And apparently Aaron had the phrase 'What have we done?' scrawled across the back of his jacket in office white-out liquid. It sounds like he's completely bonkers and to think that, compared to me at Uni, he thought of himself as some sort of saint.

I have my mad moments, but not like that. Sometimes I feel like wandering round screaming at the world, although I'm not sure what I would say. Knowing me, it would probably be 'Where have all the chocolate biscuits gone?' If anything might be the cause for genuine existential panic, a Hob-Nob shortage is.

And so Aaron was the last Christian man I dated. To be honest, my track record with guys hasn't been too good. I'm hardly what you would call a saint. Everyone sees me as the good girl, but far too often my head has been turned by some guy that I know is COMPLETELY wrong for me. Sometimes I can't even tell the guys I go out with that I am a Christian, because I know they will break up with me, especially if they know that sex is off the cards . . . It's just that I've never really fancied a Christian guy, not since Aaron anyway, and he obviously didn't think I was good enough for him. So I suppose I gave up.

My friend James, who runs the house group at church with me, is lovely, he really is. Sometimes I think it could work out between the two of us. He's so kind and caring and dependable – he's always ready to help out with the sound desk at church or whatever Robert needs. The problem with James is that I love him in a benignly Christian way, but I don't fancy him. When I think about him kissing me, it grosses me out. I know that's a horrible thing to say about somebody, (guilty Helen again) and it's not that he's ugly, or that there's anything wrong with him at all, he just doesn't DO IT for me. If I was holier I probably wouldn't care about that.

I mean, he's a Christian and lovely, so what more should I want? I know he'd completely look after me. Is it wrong to ask God to help you want to have sex with someone, or is that weird? Or maybe I'm not supposed to have those feelings before my honeymoon when God will suddenly grant us a lusty love life. I don't know! But now wonderful worship leader/boy band singer with floppy hair is on the way to Frenton.

I'm excited now and fearful and guilty in almost equal measures . . .

*God, all I want to do is do the right thing and if that means marrying James I will, because I want to serve you. Please, please, please give me a husband. I'm so lonely. Is Kristian Vivian Rogers the one? Amen.*

## WEDNESDAY JANUARY 17th

Led house group tonight with James, which was about prayer. Confessed to everyone that I do find the one-way conversation that is prayer rather hard and they seemed relieved to hear it. Told James about Kristian Vivian Rogers being appointed and for some reason blurted out that I'd seen his photo on the Internet. James didn't look impressed about my web surfing or excited about us getting a new worship leader.

It's been a tough day. I went to see Hayley and the sum total of our little chat was that she told me to go away immediately by repeatedly yelling two words (thirty five times), the second of which was 'Off'. Called Dad to offload a bit, but his mobile wasn't on; he was probably in a Council committee meeting.

I shed a couple of tears and obviously still looked upset when I got back to the office. Laura, who so far is the only person who has made an effort to befriend me there, told me in her lovely cockney accent that you never can tell with these kids. You might think that someone's as hard as old boots on the surface, but they could be as gooey as a chocolate éclair underneath. I wish that was the case with Hayley. I suspect the only thing you'd get if you got into her insides would be a pervasive smell of marijuana and the small change she'd pilfered from your back pockets.

The other thing that Laura says is that it doesn't matter if you get results or not, the point is that you do what you do because, well, it's the right thing to do. It doesn't matter whether it works or not. I thought about that, yet Jesus did loads of good things and they always seemed to get a result. I seem to get abuse or uninterest. Then I thought some more and realised that most of the good things that Jesus did actually got him rejected and into hot water and ultimately nailed to a cross.

*Lord, please help me have more effect at work, I feel like I'm banging my head against a brick wall.*

However, Laura does believe in being firm with Hayley. Laura met Hayley when she came to the office demanding money. Apparently Hayley gave her a mouthful because she had to wait in reception for twenty minutes because appointments were running late. Hayley started screaming and Laura held up her hand and said, 'Shout at this, sweetie, 'cause that's the only thing that's going to respond. Yelling won't get you anywhere here.' And at that, Hayley sat down and shut up, though the fixed scowl on her face didn't budge for twenty minutes.

Sometimes I wish I could have Laura's no-nonsense no-fear confidence, yet mingled with kindness too.

Tonight after house group I read Genesis 9, which is where Noah spent a little too long at the grape trough and ended up totally legless (felt a little relieved about my old Uni lapse) whereupon his son Ham (who was such a nasty piece of work that much pork would be named after him) made a laughing stock of his dad, whereas the other two sons, Shem and Japheth, covered their father's nakedness and preserved his dignity. Had to banish unhelpful fantasy of Mel Gibson (gorgeous and devout Catholic with it) playing legless and loincloth-less Noah in a tent and my coming svelte-like to his rescue . . . Am I the only Christian who is actually so frustrated that she's even found reading a passage in the Bible arousing? (Robert's sermon on the Song of Solomon last year was a delight in some rather unhelpful ways . . . )

Once I'd managed to send that delicious notion packing, I couldn't help thinking that some Christians are like Ham – they seem to get a real thrill out of seeing others fail and struggle. Thought about Mr and Mrs Hemming again; decided that I preferred to think about Mel in a tent.

Tired again. Have prayed for dreams that don't feature Mel in an Old Testament *Waterworld*, with Kevin Costner as Ham. But am not sure I want that prayer answered. Didn't say *amen*.

It must have been the thought of Mel and Kevin and *Waterworld*, but I suddenly remembered my dad taking me fishing from the end of the pier when I was about five. My fishing line got totally entangled around the reel and after a few seconds of trying to sort it, I handed it to Dad, who spent the next fifteen minutes carefully and patiently unpicking the knots.

*Lord, sometimes I feel overwhelmed and lost inside my own head. There are so many thoughts, motives, fears and hopes, all messed up in a bunch like a tangled fishing line. Help me, not so much to untangle the sorry mess, but to hand it over to you. Amen.*

This idea of journal honesty is being tested to the limit.

I had the strangest dream last night and when I say strange, I mean completely and utterly *weird*. Even Sigmund Freud would edge slowly and carefully away from me. I need to be instantly sectioned, covered from head to foot in holy oil produced in Israel, prayed over by nuns for 40 days and 40 nights and exorcised with a ceremony involving garlic. The dream was so sick I can't even remember it without feeling like I need the internal equivalent of a 90 degree wash. Gross. I won't repeat the sordid details, because if anyone ever found this diary I would DIE of shame. But call me Helen 'so perverse they aren't even NAMES for the things she did in her dreams last night' Sloane. And the worst thing was, I woke up and wanted to nod off immediately so that I could get back into the dream. There, I've said it, I am a pervert and should be locked up for the sake of other people's safety. Katy, one of the Riverdancing backing singers at church and a member of our house group, was talking only last night about how sometimes she wakes up praying. PRAYING! A whole tent of circus performers couldn't recreate what I woke up dreaming, even if you included the menagerie. God, please cleanse my mind so this doesn't happen again. Why can't I be like Julie Andrews or Mother Teresa or Katy? I bet they never had this problem . . .

Blah kind of work day mostly involving admin catch-ups with nothing of note to report. Before sleeping, I showered, prayed for a loooooooooooooong time (being a pervert, I need all the help I can get), read not only my daily section of the Bible, but also the one I didn't read yesterday and then, because you never know, I read tomorrow's as well. I then sang along, very badly (sorry God) with that new worship CD, *Smelling the hair of Christ* which I kept playing quietly all night. Slept fitfully but managed to avoid any more perverse dreams. Thank God for the power of prayer.

Part of my marathon Bible-reading stint was the Sodom and Gomorrah incident (Gen. 19) which describes the mad, desperate need for sex in that city and the brutality and perversity of the place. I was strangely comforted by the vile story, because I realised that I live in a sick world that's crawling with nasty ideas and images: no wonder my mind sometimes blows a fuse and dreams sicko stuff like I did the other night. On reflection, perhaps I'm not such a pervert after all. I'd assumed that journalling was supposed to make me feel bad about myself, what with all that introspection, but am now finding out that sometimes it makes me feel better. I wondered whether that happened to that crusty Simeon Stylites, the pole sitter.

*Lord, help me to live for you. The world's sometimes a horrid place and it rubs off. Amen.*

## SUNDAY JANUARY 21st

It being Sunday, as usual I attended the service at New Wave. But this was no ordinary day! It was an eventful, even epic morning, and not just because of the arrival of man of God Kristian: blessed is he who comes in the name of the Lord! K.V.Rogers, or K.V. as I called him during the entirely imaginary conversations that I had with him in my head today, is even better looking than his Google photo portrays, all fresh and blond and tanned from his outreach in the South of France.

I have no idea what kind of mission he was on, but it sounded like he was doing a lot of open air ministry, as he mentioned being on the beach a lot. What a bold, courageous, tanned, godly, tanned, spiritually sensitive, tanned young man he is! He does have one teeny-weeny imperfection. After leading worship, (wonderfully, I must say), he handed the service back to Robert, who was our preacher for the morning. But I noticed that when Kristian sat down, (on the pew in front of mine, tell me that's not God!) he put his guitar back in its stand and then sat back and didn't seem to pay any attention to what Robert said at all. He didn't open a Bible (don't think he even had one) but he started scribbling something – at first I thought that maybe he was making notes about the sermon and was concentrating hard, but then I leaned over to take a closer look and saw that he was actually writing a poem, or something like that. But then he began writing guitar chords over the words – he was writing a new worship song during dear lovely Robert's sermon, which I thought was a bit off. I tried to tell myself that Kristian is in fact a tanned King David prophetic-psalmist type whose creative muse is the preaching of the Scriptures – but if I'm honest I fear that he might be a little bit too interested in his own stuff and not terribly attentive to any teaching. But this is but a mere foible, a trifling issue compared to his immense anointing as a leader, and his perfect teeth. And did I mention his tan?

Anyway, his lack of attention was certainly his loss, because Robert's sermon was nothing short of stunning, fabulous and wonderful. In fact, it usually is. Robert is an inspiration: he's down to earth, vulnerable and funny, but always manages to nudge us to think about our faith. One or two members of our little congregation aren't so keen on him, especially Mr and Mrs Hemming. Realised when I saw them both this morning that I hadn't nursed any thoughts about murdering her lately, which might be an answer to prayer – or maybe my mind has been too preoccupied with the coming of K.V.

Mr Hemming always wears the same suit and the same frown on Sundays, as if he believes that God wants us all to assume an expression suggesting that we are suffering from severe constipation and are in need of much bran. Perhaps I should print out Mum's Caribbean explosion diet for him. And not only is Mrs Hemming such a gifted 'sharer', but she seems to love catching people doing something wrong. Actually, I need to put that differently. What Mrs Hemming actually loves doing is catching people doing things that she doesn't like, which includes singing new worship songs, using a version of the Bible that was translated in the last 300 years or so, or – the crime that is tantamount to blasphemy and deserves a burning – reorganising the chairs in what she calls 'the sanctuary'. Mr and Mrs Hemming are a walking demonstration that there is a just God out there, because they definitely deserve each other. They sat through Robert's sermon on 'Running the Race' with faces so long you'd have thought he'd announced that he was going to preach while naked. It was a fabulous message. Robert pointed out that Paul the Apostle was into sports, what will all those analogies about running and chariot racing, wrestling and boxing. Mrs Hemming definitely didn't approve and shot one of those sneery looks at her husband when Robert mentioned wrestling, which she probably lists as a carnal pursuit. I had an unholy thought about Mr and Mrs Hemming engaging in wrestling, which I swiftly banished. Anyway, Robert told us that the Christian life calls for faithfulness and discipline. I was instantly challenged, which I sometimes think is Christian code for feeling bad.

My lack of good discipline *is* an issue and my chocolate biscuit problem obviously needs a firm hand, there being no support groups like Alcoholics Anonymous: 'Hi, I'm Helen and I'm addicted to Hob Nobs . . . '

So . . .

I have decided to literally run the race. Yes, I, Helen Sloane, am going to run a marathon this year. Training begins tomorrow. I shall decide on a good cause, pester my friends for sponsorship, raise some pounds in cash, lose some pounds in fat and become a woman in control of her life.

There were a couple of other happenings in the service. I went forward for prayer in response to Robert's sermon, to make firm my determination to become a marathoner. But then my mind wandered during the prayer. James came out to the front and stood with me while I was being prayed for, which was lovely, but I couldn't help thinking about a bronzed, blond psalmist of the Lord during the praying. He was strumming his guitar quietly during the prayer, providing a sort of divine backing music and everyone started singing a worship song that talked about 'kissing the Lord with our praises'. Unfortunately I found myself singing the song while thinking about snogging luscious Kristian. And then, to make it worse, when the prayer was over James swept me into one of those 'Oh I love you in the Lord most precious sister' hugs, which lasted two or three seconds longer than it probably needed to and I felt even more guilty about my longings for closer fellowship with our new worship leader. I was preparing myself for a major guilt session as we moved into sharing communion, which then helpfully turned out to be completely hilarious and distracted me from too much breast-smiting.

Mrs Hemming is in charge of preparing the bread and wine and she guards that responsibility like a rottweiller on crack. She threatened to leave the church last year when Robert suggested that a rota be created so that others could share the privilege. She said that this was her God-given ministry in the fellowship and nobody was going to take it away from her. After all, she said, women should not preach (it's not what our church believes, just Mr and Mrs Hemming, because they think that females are likely to lead the brethren astray just as Eve did with her shapely hips and good-looking apple). So, Mrs H argued, this was her way of serving the Lord.

Apparently Mrs Hemming hadn't realised that all the wine had been used last week. She believes that Sunday shopping is going to earn wayward Sabbath breakers an eternal grilling on God's hellish barbecue, so she refused to allow anyone to go to the shops to get some more. The only thing available was some raspberry jelly left over from the Prime Timers OAP Christmas party, so Mrs Hemming announced that the Lord had truly provided, diluted the jelly sufficiently (or so she thought) and poured the purple concoction into those little cups and placed the trays of holy jelly under the white doilies on the communion table. Sadly (or perhaps providentially) Robert's sermon was quite long, the prayer time after it took longer than usual because so many people responded and so, by the time we got to taking communion, it had set solid. It's tough trying to reverently scoop up such a holy emblem with one's little finger. One lad at the back who was obviously too young to partake loudly asked where the fruit salad and ice cream was. But it was a wonderful moment, mainly because Mrs Hemming looked fit to bust.

A sad postscript though: Mr Hemming got into a row with Robert right after the service. It was Robert's fault, said Mr Hemming, that his wife had been so mortally embarrassed by the setting jelly. His sermons should be shorter and what was the need for times of prayer anyway? Robert tried to respond, but in the end I think he gave up. Sometimes religious people lose the capacity to listen.

Anyway, I am now a marathon runner in training, an athlete on their way to sporting glory, like Eric Liddell of *Chariots of Fire* fame. Step aside, Keira, here I come . . .

## MONDAY JANUARY 22nd

What a morning! I felt a little discouraged that oxygen seemed so very elusive after just half a mile of running, but even Eric Liddell started somewhere. I told Laura at work about my marathon decision. She's a runner, so she gave me some great advice. 'Just decide, Helen. Decide that, from now on, there's no ifs, buts or excuses. No discussion allowed in your head. Just run. Every day.'

I got to my desk to be greeted by a work avalanche. It seems like every child care case in Frenton landed on my desk over the weekend. Then I went over to Hayley's aunt and uncle's this afternoon. Hayley was out at the shops so I had to sit and wait for her. It was difficult to chat to Hayley's aunt, as she talks endlessly and doesn't think listening is part of a conversation. Not only that, but she'd been drinking; the sour smell of whisky made my stomach turn.

'You're a blimmin' inferring cow.' Hayley's aunt glared at me as she chugged on what was, judging by the overflowing ashtray on the coffee table, her ten millionth Mayfair cigarette that afternoon.

'You social workers, you're always sticking your nose in, aren't yer? You know better than everyone else, don't yer, Miss stuck-up duffel-coat lady?'

She paused to cough and enjoy the fruits of her lifelong investment in the Mayfair tobacco company.

'We don't need your help, you hear? We're alright. Hayley's high-spirited, that's all. All kids are like that. I used to be like Hayley and I turned out okay.'

Thought about that statement and put together a reply but decided not to share it . . .

'Mrs Tennant' I tried to reply politely, 'not all teenagers tie flaming pieces of rubbish onto the tail of a dog and push the poor creature through their neighbour's windows whilst screaming "Release the hounds!"'

I had to pause again to allow Mrs Tennant space for a good minute's rasping coughing, as well as a couple more puffs.

'I know Hayley has had a difficult home life and I am trying to ensure there's a more stable environment for her so she can overcome these behavioural problems.'

With that, Hayley stomped through the door, an expression of complete thunder on her face, took one look at me and shared a warm greeting.

'Yo, it's the stuck-up bitch from the Council.'

'Excuse *me*', I replied, trying to reinstate my authority and show that I'm not scared of these two maniac women and praying of course in my head that God would grant me the power of some über-angel, so I could turn them both into pillars of salt.

But apparently I couldn't summon up an intimidating enough pose because Hayley let rip and it wasn't pretty. I'd write it down in here, but frankly the presence of all those profanities might turn these pages blue. The long and the short of it was that by denying Hayley Christmas with her family, I had also denied her a new Game Boy, an MP3 player, a mobile phone, Britney Spear's new perfume and goodness knows what other clothes and gadgets. Apparently her mum and dad like to make up for their complete lack of parental care and responsibility by lavishing her with things (which they probably can't afford and must go on their credit cards). Now Hayley can't possibly show her face in public because her mobile phone is a whole six months effing old and her effing MP3 player only holds eight hundred songs and she needs to download the whole of P Diddy's back catalogue from a mate's Ipod. I've seriously considered giving up social work for good today . . .

*Lord, the worst thing was this: I was actually frightened of her. I was terrified of a sixteen-year-old kid. As a Christian, I know I'm supposed to be all confident in you and have faith that you will protect me in that kind of situation. But to be honest, I couldn't get out of there fast enough. Her aunt was probably too drunk to hit me that hard, but Hayley, she looked like once she'd started she'd never stop. That poor, strange frightening little girl . . .*

*When I'm in a church service it all seems so easy to have faith in you. When I'm praying, I'm full of all these fantasies about being some sort of Christian Buffy the Vampire Slayer, who, when confronted with situations like that, ends up rebuking the hatred in Jesus' name, saying something incredibly* meaningful and profound and leading the whole room to Christ. It always seems to work in the Bible: why doesn't it ever seem to work today?

As I left, I wondered what kind of person Hayley might have been if she'd been brought up with some basics like love and security. How different would she have been if her parents had talked to her?

And all that musing about the power of love and relationships got me thinking about my confession the other day about sex, and I've realised it's not just sex that I want. Well, obviously, yes, I definitely want the sex. But it's more about the intimacy that surrounds sex. You know, those long mornings snuggled up in bed, having pillow fights and feeding each other strawberries. Okay! I've seen far too many movies, but something vaguely along those lines would be great. I mean, it's hard to be alone and not have that kind of intimacy with anyone. I think that's what humans were made for. After all, Adam was supposed to have had a perfect relationship with God, yet he still wanted the intimacy with Eve that companionship brings. Snuggling up and teasing each other with what I'm sure will be hilariously witty banter; having someone hug you and hug you without it becoming awkward and a bit embarrassing. Plus, they'd be someone to make you tea in the mornings and perhaps even bring you a couple of chocolate biscuits. Sounds like heaven to me . . .

*God, please bless and guide and preserve Kristian. May he settle into our church easily and develop one or two good, close, loving friendships very quickly. Or maybe just one of those good, close and loving friendships would be sufficient. Amen.*

Wondered if there was a strawberry patch in Eden. Or music.

Didn't manage to run at all today . . . must get Laura to give me her little speech again. And must sort out which charity I am going to run for . . .

Horrific news! My 56-year-old mother has pierced her nose. Yes, my 56-year-old, Chanel No. 5-wearing mother went to the tattoo and piercing parlour and got her nose punctured by someone called Killer, who apparently was very nice, despite having a tattoo of a snake strangling a kitten on his forearm. Apparently the crystal nose-stud 'projects' her nasal ley line so it can 'interact' with her moon-star chakra, which (according to her best friend Babs) will make sure that nothing bad ever happens to her again, ever, period. You also have to send £50 to some guru called Bshach Yabba, who lives in a permanent state of serenity in India. Babs has returned from her own personal pilgrimage to India and apparently it was very relaxing, apart from (according to her) 'those nasty little beggar children putting their grubby fingers over my prayer shawl'. God forbid that the poor of the earth might hijack Bab's odd spirituality . . .

The worst thing about my mother's nose-piercing is that it doesn't actually look too bad. She may be 56, but I strongly suspect she is more attractive than me. She certainly dresses better. Last week she was wearing skinny jeans, yes, I said *my mother wears skinny jeans!* I can't even pull off skinny jeans. Or more precisely, I can't even pull *on* skinny jeans. Not past my knees anyway.

My parents live in a quaint little village outside of Frenton which has a Post Office that only opens once a month. The village is very picturesque, horribly boring but pretty in a

Beatrix Potterish kind of way. Mum and Dad live in a cottage designed for hobbits, specifically hobbits with a penchant for hanging crystals and wind chimes swinging from every available outdoor surface. When the wind blows, it sounds like an explosion in a glass factory.

Speaking of chimes, my parents are both Christians and they attend the local village church. Dad seems to get it and he's been a support to the local vicar, lending a hand with the accounts when the church's somewhat elderly church treasurer unfortunately and suddenly disappeared with a woman thirty years his junior, a hairdresser called Tracey. Dad and I have had some great chats about God; he knows the Bible really well. He's not loud about faith though and he does seem to have a bit of a blind spot when it comes to my mum, because she doesn't seem to get Christianity at all. She believes in God, but sometimes she gives me the impression that her belief is in whatever god of the week is in vogue. She thinks that all spirituality is fine, as long as it involves vaguely being nice to each other and incense. She's not sure what a religion should contain, but if it doesn't involve setting fire to things that smell nice and funny mumbling, then she's not interested.

I wish Dad would talk to her about it more and help put her on the straight and narrow, but he doesn't. I think that the poor man is hopelessly besotted with her and believes that she'll sort it all out in her own way and time.

All of which means that when Mum mentioned her new crystal nasal appendage on the phone this morning, I decided to pop round for a viewing tonight and perhaps have a chat about her pick'n'mix spirituality.

I let myself in, banged my head on the hobbit door frame and called 'Mum? Dad? Are you around?'

'Daaaarling, is that you?' Mum's voice echoed down the hallway. 'Come up here. I'm in the bath, so pop yourself down and let's have a nice chat.'

When I was younger most of the quality time between my mum and I was spent in the bathroom, with me perched on the closed toilet lid whilst my mother luxuriated in the bath, sandalwood aromatherapy candle flickering, gripping a glass of red wine with her perfectly manicured fingernails.

'Look, daaarling, look, look what mummy Kitty's done! I've gone and pierced my nose, how naughty am I?!'

My mother keeps trying to get me to call her Kitty like all her friends do. She says the word 'Mother' makes her feel old. I love her desperately, but want her to stay in her current role as my mum and not turn me into another one of her friends in the 'ladies that lunch' set . . .

'Darling, you look tired. I do hope you've not been overdoing it. You could do with some fun! Tell you what, I'll take you shopping next weekend . . . '

And then she went on about how Babs was a brand new person as a result of her Indian epiphany and that she's going to London next week for a colonic irrigation, because apparently all that purging helps you focus . . .

We nattered back and forth happily because, despite my mum being so inter-galactic, she always seems to realise in time that she's been chuntering on, and makes room for me to chat – which is nice, but also creates a problem, which I'll try to explain in a moment . . .

Then suddenly and without warning, my mother gets out the bath, with, as-per-usual, absolutely no modesty whatsoever. I get horribly embarrassed every time she strides around naked, which is frequently, often when she's doing the housework. She tried to get my father to join a naturist group once: thank God, he refused, and she said there was no point going without him. She hates doing things without my dad. Though I like to think my desperate prayers had something to do with it.

Anyway, she's sitting on the edge of the bath wrapped in a towel (another answered prayer) and I wanted to tell her about the three people who are making me lose sleep at the moment – nightmare Hayley, who sometimes appears in dreams that feature teenagers armed with chainsaws, and Mr and Mrs Hemming, who use the Bible like a chainsaw. I'm not sure which of these oh-so difficult people upsets me more.

But here's the problem – with Mum somewhat up in the air about her faith (sometimes she's not so much as high as a kite as cruising at 36,000 feet like a jumbo jet) – I feel reluctant to tell her about my struggles. I worry that she'll think that my faith in Jesus doesn't work (thus nudging her towards ever more weird spiritual safaris) or that the church is full of hypocrites (once again nudging her towards ever more weird spiritual safaris). And so when she asks me how I'm doing, I lie and say I'm fine: the job's demanding, I say and leave it at that. Bizarrely, because I don't want to let the side down, I end up being dishonest with my own mother and that creates obvious distance between us, at least from my side. And I think she senses that I'm not letting her into my struggles, which worries me, because I'd hate to hurt her.

I do so love her, even though her willowy body (even when naked) makes me envious. If my body was a tree, it wouldn't be a willow – it's more like an oak. And 'oaky' isn't a good description for anything except Chardonnay.

Mum bustled off to dry her hair and I hate trying to continue a chat with a 900 watt turbo dryer on at full blast, because it means shouting. So I took the opportunity to wander off to find my dad. Mum says that he's on one of his little campaigns.

'He's at it again, darling. You now how upset he got over the' (and here she mouthed the words silently, as if mentioning the unmentionable) '*battle of the beach-huts* affair . . . well now he's fighting another just war . . . '

The battle of the beach-huts is a campaign that we don't like to talk about much in our house. My father is a retired bank manager but, as I said, he also works part time for the local government as a Councillor. A couple of years ago, there was a big scandal involving a proposal to build new beach huts. They were going to be located down a stretch of beach that was completely unsuitable: there were no toilets, no proper parking and apparently, in the winter, the tide could be so severe that it might even wash them away. There was one Councillor whose family business was a building company and he wanted to give his brother permission to build on this stretch of beach so they could sell the huts off at an extortionate price to unsuspecting citizens. My father found out about the nasty little scheme and went mad. He tried to generate a community-wide protest against the blatant corruption but ended up not only losing the debate (the Council flexed its muscles and Dad suspects some under-the counter political deals) but he almost had to give up his seat because of it.

Dad's such a mild-mannered man and I don't think he's sore for himself because he lost – it's that he hates it when the fat cats win. He says that he spent a lifetime as a banker in the city watching the big boys throw their weight around and lobbing people's lives onto the scrapheap for the sake of a fast buck and so now when he sees that kind of behaviour in our community, he'll half-kill himself to fight it.

I wandered into his study and found him with his nose in a law-book, obviously preparing for his next battle. It's amazing how little actions can make someone so completely lovable. As I walked in, Dad put his book down and closed it without putting a bookmark in it and stood up to give me a hug. It's a genuine gesture that makes me feel like I'm the exclusive focus of his attention. I feel a bit guilty now as I look back on the moment, because I didn't even ask him about his new battle, but launched almost immediately into my woes about the Hemmings and Hayley.

He smiled and nodded and I'm sure that at one point he wiped away a tear. I wasn't sure whether that was for Hayley, because she's been so messed up, or for me, because he can see that I'm stretched to the limit.

Then he said, 'It's tough, darling, when you're investing in the invisible. And that's what you do when you pour yourself into other people's lives: there's no gauge that says that they're listening, that they care what you think, that anything you're doing is helpful. You don't win every battle and sometimes, you don't win any. But people are worth fighting for. Keep going with Hayley. Sometimes icebergs take almost forever to thaw. And don't fret about the Hemmings, because a dose of religion is no guarantee that irritating and stupid people will be less irritating and stupid.'

I'd like to say that I fully imbibed this wisdom, but any time anyone mentions icebergs I think of Leonardo Di Caprio and then go off into a daydream, drooling gently . . .

Didn't feel hugely inspired to become Queen of the world, à la Kate and Leonardo, as a result of my chat with Dad, but did decide (a) not to abandon social work in order to embrace new career as a fuller-figure supermodel and (b) not to kill anyone with an 'H' in their name, like Hemming or Hayley.

## WEDNESDAY JANUARY 24th

Can only write one line today and it's urgent and desperate. *Please, please, please God, I'll do anything – but let Hayley be found safely. Please. Amen. Please.*

## THURSDAY JANUARY 25th

More of the same. She's still missing. The police are involved now. *Please. Please.*

## FRIDAY JANUARY 26th

Okay, some explanations. Wednesday I got a phone call from Hayley's hideous aunt telling me that Hayley hadn't come home. Apparently she went out to see some friends – they tend to hang around by the pier and eat bags of chips – but she didn't come back at the end of the evening. She's not answering her mobile phone, none of her friends that the police have contacted so far have any idea where she is – or if they do, they're not saying – and the police are drawing a blank. When her aunt phoned today, she clearly implied that Hayley is missing because I've been negligent in some way and haven't provided Hayley with the support that she needs, which is so wrong . . . and yet . . . because I'm so good at guilt, I worry that perhaps I haven't done everything right and that I might have allowed Hayley's abusive tirades to lessen my professional care for her. I've even gone through her case notes three times to check on the frequencies of my home visits and make sure that I kept all the appointments that I made with her. And I did. But I still feel that somehow I might be to blame. Did I leave their house too early the other day because I was scared? If I'd stayed a little longer, might there have been a conversation that could have prevented Hayley from going missing?

*Please God, let her be found. The police are talking about putting posters around the town with her photograph on. Please, please God.*

Tonight James and Vanessa came out to walk around the town with me, in the vain hope that we might find her hanging out with one of the gaggle of kids who horse around in the streets. James was great and was quite bold. I felt nervous about approaching one group of older kids, who looked stoned and bolshy, to ask if they knew Hayley – so James marched right up to them and managed a chat with no problem. They didn't know her, but I thought that it was nice of James to put himself out like that. And then Vanessa was lovely too. She was praying out loud, quietly but continuously, as we walked around the town. She can be so very mad and odd and yet it was wonderfully comforting to hear her whispering her prayers while we walked. It kept reminding me that we are not on our own in times like this. Thank God for God – and thank God for friends.

*Please God, may Hayley be found. Keep her safe and I'll do everything I can to help her, if you'll give me wisdom. Amen.*

## SATURDAY JANUARY 27th

Hayley is a selfish, obnoxious little cow and I don't like her one bit. She showed up at her house last night and seemed completely amazed about all the fuss. Apparently she got chatting to an older lad at the pier last Tuesday night – and they stayed chatting after all of her other friends had gone home. He lives in a caravan on one of the residential sites here and so when he invited her back for the night, she agreed and basically hung out with him doing Lord knows what for the last three days and only came home last night because she'd run out of money and he was skint. I went to see her this afternoon and she was horrible, refused to tell me what she and her boyfriend had been up to and in fact barely spoke to me at all. She answered every question I asked her with the same response.

Why did you go with him?

*I'm bored.*

Didn't you think that everyone would be worried about you?

*I'm bored.*

Did he hurt you?

*Everything's boring.*

What can I do to help you, Hayley?

*Why not shut up for a start? You're soooo boring.*

For thirty minutes Hayley said the same thing over and over again and then it hit me.

She's bored.

When I got back to the office, I had a little chat with Laura about it, who says that something needs to be done for all these kids who hang out at the pier. The streets at night are a dangerous place to be, Laura says. Something needs to be done to take them off the streets and give them some safe, alternative things to do. Someone needs to do something. That might not solve all of the problems of someone like Hayley, but it would be a start. It might stop some other kids ending up with bigger issues than they have already.

She's right.

## SUNDAY JANUARY 28th

I read Exodus 29 this morning, which is about Aaron being chosen and anointed as a priest. I wondered what it would be like to be picked out by God to do something special . . .

Church was good this morning. Mrs Hemming was complaining again (loudly, so almost everyone could hear) over the after-service cup of tea. She hated Robert's sermon and told him so, using the weapon that is always guaranteed to devastate: 'We're not being fed in this church.' It's so difficult to defend yourself against that one.

And then something rather wonderful happened, a small victory. Nola, Robert's wife, is always so warm and kind, but there was a flash of something wild in her eyes as she strode over to Robert and Mrs H. She took Mrs Hemming's empty tea cup with a little more force than was necessary, which was marvellous, and then spoke up.

'I wonder if you really managed to catch everything he was saying, Mrs Hemming, or to appreciate the amount of study and preparation that went into it. You did appear to be talking to your husband through most of it, so perhaps you didn't hear that much?'

And with that, Nola swept away, leaving Mrs Hemming speechless, which is a miracle on a par with Lazarus coming out of his tomb. I love Nola.

I wondered up to Kristian, almost barged one of the Barbie doll worship backing singers out of the way, and introduced myself.

'Nice to meet you, Hel' he said.

I smiled and said, ever so gently, that my name was Helen, but he obviously didn't get my point, because he went into a three minute monologue about how he's enjoying the church and how this week he managed to write three new songs and kept calling me 'Hel' throughout it.

Noone calls me Hel. I hate being called Hel. I don't want people to think of me and subliminally connect my personality with eternal conscious torment, which is how Mrs Hemming describes that place. I'm sure I'll eventually be able to teach Kristian to call me something else. Like honey. Darling would be fine.

I thought again about my chat with Laura and the pier kids. Prayed once more that someone would do something about them.

## MONDAY JANUARY 29th

Prayed again that someone would do something for these kids.

## WEDNESDAY JANUARY 31st

Suggested to James that we spend some time at the house group praying that someone would do something for the kids. He agreed that we should and so we did. During the prayer, Katy said she had a picture of a pier that had been devastated by a storm and half of it had been swept away. Some of the group thought that this meant that the kids had been so damaged by the storms of life. I quietly thought that this was mad because (a) that's obvious and (b) Frenton *does* have a pier that has been devastated by a storm and half of it has been swept away. Sometimes my fellow Christians make me wonder . . .

. . . has all the maniacal jigging done by Katy and the worship backing girlies done something to their brains?

## THURSDAY FEBRUARY 1st

Decided that perhaps I should do something about these kids.

I can't.

I'm too busy.

I'm already involved in too much.

I scarcely have any time for myself as it is. I got together with

Vanessa tonight, with a view of talking it all out. It was a great evening. After the dreadful few days of worry about Hayley going missing, it was good to be a bit giggly and silly. That's what great about Vanessa – she may be odd but she's a laugh. We also had a good pray as well and spent some time thanking God for Hayley being safe – am now able to pray that and mean it. We had a deep chat about prayer too. I've decided that unanswered prayer isn't the problem – it's answered prayer that is the real challenge.

With children dying everyday in Africa – isn't any request from us relatively rich people in the West a bit frivolous and low on God's list of priorities? Why should God bother with any of it? I struggle sometimes with the thought that it's perhaps even mildly obscene that we talk to him about our money, coughs and colds, choice of car, who we'll marry and a thousand and one other comparative trivialities. And yet God is interested.

Then, as V and I chatted, I felt selfish because I brought it all back down to me. I'm ashamed to admit it, but it niggles me a bit to realize that God did apparently answer our prayers about missing motormouth Hayley, but all my fervent intercessions about my love life have taken me nowhere.

Then we got talking about the problem of bored kids in Frenton and Vanessa grabbed my hand and said we needed to pray about it, right now. It was an urgent matter, she said. God loves these kids, she said. Someone needs to do something for these kids, she said.

We prayed. But I already knew. *I'm* going to do something for these kids.

Nice weekend. Had another 7 minute chat with Kristian after the service yesterday morning, when he asked me repeatedly how I felt he was doing as the church's new worship leader. 'It's a difficult gig, Hel' he said. 'Creativity needs context and I'm still settling in and sometimes I feel a bit awkward, a bit closed in. Besides, Robert is insisting that the sung worship part of the service should only last 30 minutes, which I feel could stifle things a bit. I need that amount of time to get into the flow, you know what I mean, Hel?'

I felt a bit uncomfortable with him criticising Robert like that – Kristian's welcome to his opinions, but I was concerned that he wasn't showing much loyalty to the team he's a part of – and he's a newcomer. Also, I think that Robert is right. Kristian tends to only use two or three songs during the half-hour set; he sings them over and over again until they become boring. And then, in between the songs, he stands there, eyes half open, nodding and smiling as if God and he are having a little chat, while the rest of us look on.

I tried to gently say something about how it's better to make good use of the time we've got, rather than steal time from the sermon, but Kristian didn't appear to be listening and seemed to think that the more we sing, the happier God gets.

'God is looking for fervent, intense worship, Hel', he said, smiling and nodding again like he does in between songs. I was worried that, mid-chat, he was going to pop off to some kind of ecstatic place where only he and Jesus can go and that this would lead to an embarrassing lull in our conversation. I also worried that he would call me 'Hel' for the fourth time and so I excused myself and left. He's a little odd, but I'm sure that his foibles could be sorted. What that man needs is a good woman at his side and maybe a short theology course. I'd be happy to help. I spent most of the rest of today sleeping and dreaming about running the marathon.

## MONDAY FEBRUARY 5th

I saw Mr Hemming on the Prom this morning, when I was running my three miles, and waved at him. He didn't wave back: he didn't even smile.

Called Vanessa on the way to work this morning to say 'Hi' and casually mentioned that I'm irritated not to be losing weight faster. Vanessa said, kindly but firmly, that she was worried about me, that I'm being superficial about my weight obsession and that, anyway, the Bible says that the body is wasting away. 'That's my problem', I said – 'I'm not so much wasting away as moving into a significant programme of expansion.' Agreed to carry on conversation over lunch (must eat fish and chips in order to impress Vanessa that I care not about the proportions of the flesh).

Yikes. Lord, what do I do? My mother texted me mid-afternoon and wants to meet my friends from church. The problem is that I don't particularly want my friends from church to meet my mother. I love her dearly, but what if she decides to cleanse their chakras over the roast chicken? She also keeps going on about how she wants to meet 'that nice man James that you run that church group thingy meeting with.' Sometimes my mother has the tact of a nuclear warhead. I wouldn't be surprised if she tried to marry us right there and then, over the carrots. Still, maybe it would be good for her to be around more 'real' Christians. Perhaps they might be able to get through all that incense smoke in a way that I can't.

Vanessa phoned and we chatted some more about the pier crowd. Vanessa suggested that a youth club might be a good way to start – the last one we had in town closed down six months ago because there was a terrible fight there. The club idea sounds good to me.

I am also now in a panic, because I have accidentally invited Vanessa to Sunday lunch with my parents. The problem with Vanessa is that, like my dad, she's actually a good listener. I was rabbiting on about something or other and before I knew it I told her how my mum wants to meet some of my church friends. Vanessa instantly agreed that was a great idea and, before I could say anything, asked whether next Sunday was what my mum had in mind.

She then said that she would phone James straight away and invite him to come too, as she could tell that I was busy. That girl is such a matchmaker . . .

*Lord, please don't let my mother make everybody eat with their hands, like she did at Auntie Gillian's last year. Palms are not adequate receptacles for soup. Lord, stay very, very close to me this week. And especially next Sunday . . .*

## TUESDAY FEBRUARY 6th

I had a thoroughly dull and boring day of back to back meetings and then attended a numbing training session about case protocols. The day was punctuated only by fears about the weekend and lunching with the parents. The final nail in the hideous coffin that was this foul Tuesday was driven in when I got home. A letter from Mrs Hemming was waiting for me. I knew it was from her, she always puts a 'God is love' sticker on everything she sends and she's written to me before, when she and Mr Hemming resigned from our house group, which was a day of great joy and celebration.

Anyway, I opened the letter with the sinking heart of a condemned woman, knowing that this would not be good. I was right.

*Dear Helen*

*Greetings in the unchanging name of our Lord (Heb. 13:8).*

*I am writing to you today as an act of faithfulness (Num. 12:7, Luke 16:10). I do this with much sorrow, (2 Cor. 7:9) but even the deeply unreliable New International Version says that 'wounds from a friend can be trusted' – or more accurately, as the King James puts it, 'faithful are the wounds of a friend' (Prov. 27:6). I am very concerned about your decision to train for the marathon. Paul the apostle clearly teaches us that 'bodily exercise profiteth little' (1 Tim. 4:8) and I am fearful that you are being distracted away from what should be real priority in your life, which is to seek first the Kingdom of God (Mt. 6:33).*

*My fears were confirmed, Helen, when my dear husband informed me that, during his prayer walk along the promenade today, he happened (is there such a thing as coincidence? Prov. 3:5) to see you out running. He tells me that he briefly glanced at you as you went running by in your red and blue lycra running clothes (with blue trim and yellow emblems that fitted very snugly around your bottom) and that while his momentary observation of you wearing such unsuitable attire was ended as he averted his eyes (Job 31:1), he was somewhat concerned that you might be seen by other men in the church who are less mature than he (Phil. 3:15) and then they would be led into carnal lustings (2 Cor. 11:3).*

*Have you prayed about this? Are you aware that anything that makes others stumble is wrong (Rom. 14:13)?*

*I pray that the eyes of your heart may be enlightened (Eph. 1:18) to see the truth (John 8:32) and that you will truly and sincerely come to the place of fruitful repentance (Matt. 3:8).*

*I speak as a faithful watchperson of the Lord (Ezek. 3:17) and because I love you in Jesus.*

*Yours cordially in Christ*
*Joan Hemming*

My response was to use some of the words that Hayley has taught me in the advanced profanity class that is our relationship.

Finally I saw sense and called Robert. I felt bad, because it was late, but he said he didn't mind. I read him Mrs Hemming's letter and he sighed a long sigh when I got to the end. And then he said, very firmly, that she was wrong. He said that some people tell others not to do things because 'they make the weaker brother stumble' but they're not vulnerable, new Christians who are easily offended, but manipulative control freaks who use the stumbling teaching as a way of controlling others and spreading their legalism. He said that health and sports were valuable and that Paul was simply trying to encourage us to keep our lives in balance and not neglect prayer and the Bible. And then he said that, as long as I wasn't being provocative, my running gear was fine and that Mr Hemming's problem was his problem and not mine. Then he laughed and said that he'd noticed that Mr Hemming's momentary glance didn't seem that momentary, from the detailed description Mrs Hemming gave in her letter.

But although I felt better after I'd chatted with Robert, I felt a bit sad for him after I'd put the phone down. Mr Hemming is his chief deacon, after all. He may irritate me, but he and his gruesome wife are a constant thorn in Robert's side. Prayed for Robert and Nola, that God will give them strength. And patience. And courage. I thought for a moment about asking God to kill the Hemmings, (slowly) but I'm sure that whole 'God is love' thing means I shouldn't.

## SATURDAY FEBRUARY 10th

Rats! I think I may have a broken washing machine and if it floods and ruins this flat, I am going to have a fit. I love my flat and have felt great coming home to it, ever since I moved in recently. I know it's not the hugest space in the world and it only has one bedroom, but I feel perfectly safe and at home here. I used to live in a crummy bed-sit by the beach, that I took for the overly romantic reason that I might hear the waves in the morning, but all I could hear was traffic and people yelling at each other.

One evening my father came to visit me there – I was feeling depressed at the time. The damp in the place had managed to creep up three of the four walls and had even managed to turn my trainers a strange shade of green. My bedding was actually wet to the touch and all my clothes smelled like they had been cursed by the bog fairy and left in the washing machine for two years. My dad came round, saw what a state the flat was in, saw what a state I was in and offered to help with a deposit for my own place. I'd like to say that I of course immediately refused, because as an independent woman I wanted to make my own way in the world without anybody's help etc etc. But the truth was that I instantly flung myself down on the floor at my father's feet and said 'YES! YES! Thank you Daddy, I'll never be bad again.'

Then I jumped up, screamed and starting singing the only song I have ever composed. It went something along the lines of:

> 'I'm getting a flat
> I'm getting a flat.
> Hold on to your hat,
> Helen's getting a flat.'

Hardly the domed cathedral height of genius, but I must admit it was catchy and I sang it in the shower for days. This flat was the first one we looked at and I instantly fell in love with it. My father went around knocking on floorboards and unscrewing the shower head whilst I laid down in the middle of the floor and proclaimed, 'Give me this flat, or give me death!', at which the estate agent seemed to back away a little faster than necessary. I feel so blessed, especially because even though my parents aren't desperately poor, they aren't rolling in money and it was a big sacrifice for them to do this for me.

Anyway, I was trying to figure out the trouble-shooting section of the washing machine manual that was obviously written by a five-year-old after consuming a sweet shop of e-numbers. In the end I gave up and phoned James, who came round right away, interpreted the foreign tongue of the manual in a jiffy, pressed a reset button somewhere in the bowels of the machine and now it's working fine. Was I wrong to call on James like that? I know he came running because of what he feels for me – so I feel a little bit manipulative. On the other hand, he seemed delighted to do it and after all, a girl needs clean clothes.

*Thank you, Lord, for James: a very nice friend. And thanks for my parents. You've been so good to me. May my mother behave tomorrow. Amen.*

## SUNDAY FEBRUARY 11th

What a day!

Went to New Wave this morning as usual.

Robert's sermon on prayer was good, especially the bit where he told us that sometimes his mind wanders and he ends up praying for the characters in *Eastenders* to get themselves sorted, which would truly be a miracle. Mrs Hemming grunted when he mentioned *Eastenders* and shot her husband a look that gave the impression that she'd never heard of such a new-fangled and indeed worldly invention as a television. Nola, Robert's wife, did a solo this morning, which was great. She's such a smiling, calm, normal lady – she works part time as a philosophy lecturer at the local community college. And, blissfully, she's not afraid of Mrs Hemming, who looked sullen all the way through Nola's piece. Her song was great: not all warbling and shrieking like some pseudo-operatic solos in church.

Kristian did a great job in leading worship, although I didn't think it was necessary to sing the refrain of the last song thirteen times and I wish he wouldn't talk so much in between the songs. He seems to have transitioned from being a happy mystic to being a verbose sage. He's still gorgeous, but even more gorgeous when he's being quiet. I was surprised to find that I was too busy worrying about the parental lunch to come to focus much on drooling over him.

After the service I thanked Nola for her song and told her about the youth club idea. She said it sounded fantastic, but a lot of hard work and asked if she, Robert or the church could do anything to help. I also told her about how I was off to Sunday lunch with Vanessa and James and Mum and Dad and asked her to pray that it would go alright. She winked and said she'd put in some fervent overtime. As we came out of the church James opened the car door for me, which was nice and we drove over to Infusion and Vanessa came bounding out, enthusing about their service and insisting that 'God had really showed up.' I confess to hating the 'God showed up' phrase, which makes God sound like an unexpected and disagreeable relative 'showing up' for Christmas, like my Uncle Ron with the ill-fitting dentures who came unannounced last year and brought hideous presents and his terrible flatulence problem with him.

When we got to the hobbit cottage my father met us at the door, wearing the same crinkled suit I had last seen him wear at Great-Aunt Margery's funeral seven years ago. My mother had obviously told him to make an effort for my friends, which was actually very kind of her and nice of him too, to be so compliant. I know he hates suits, having been sentenced to wear one in the city every day for decades.

James banged his head on the door frame, as did I, though Vanessa seemed to glide her way effortlessly through. My mother insisted on kissing and hugging us all, even though this was the first time she had met either Vanessa or James. I swear she pressed that boy to her bosom for a little longer than necessary and he looked like he was going to faint with embarrassment. Vanessa, on the other hand, loves huggy stuff like that and it was actually my mother who eventually had to prise her off like a limpet.

'Call me Kitty', my Mother cooed at them, giving James a saucy wink. 'I've opened a bottle of champagne because it's not often I get to meet Helen's lovely friends.'

I suddenly panicked. You see, it's the drinking.

Neither Vanessa nor James drinks at all. We're talking not even a sip of port at Christmas. I wouldn't be surprised if James even refused brandy butter on his Christmas pudding. As for Vanessa, I think everybody's secretly relieved that she doesn't drink. Vanessa drunk would be even barmier than she is now. She'd probably start seeing angels and demons and visions of the future.

Actually, apparently she sees that stuff already, but this would probably be in technicolour, as opposed to the fuzzy pictures she currently views. I admit that James would probably be marginally more exciting after liberal amounts of alcohol. Maybe if we did get married I could sneak some into the water supply. It might liven things up.

My parents however, are quite big drinkers. They're not alcoholics, but if there was no wine on the table at dinner, I'd be worried my parents had been replaced by robotic clones from the future or something.

Vanessa and James refused the champagne and I was left in a real quandary. If I said 'No' to the champagne, (which I wanted), it would make my mother feel bad. I noticed that it was a bottle my parents had brought back from France last year and saved for a special occasion.

Perhaps my mother was thinking that I was going to announce my engagement to James! Whatever the reason, she had made a real effort and I didn't want to hurt her and yet I didn't want to look like an alcoholic in front of Vanessa and James.

In the end I took a small glass, protesting as she filled it all the way to the top. But it seemed to make her happy and it's only a glass of champagne, for goodness sake. James gave me a strange look but Vanessa didn't even seem to notice. She was wandering around the room picking up ornaments and peering into corners. I swear she started to tell the little china elephant on the coffee table about the resurrection of Jesus and how that affects its little elephant life.

My mother poured another liberal glass for herself and announced that, despite all previous precedents, dinner was in fact ready and on time. As we walked into the dining-room I was blown away. My mum had made a beautiful roast dinner with all the trimmings, lit candles and had even put fresh flowers and decorations on the table. It suddenly hit me that despite my mum's slight craziness, she's always made a real effort to look after me and be interested in my life; and she shows it by being someone who does all the details. I remember when I was eight I desperately wanted to go as Cinderella to a fancy dress party and my mother spent weeks sewing frills onto masses of petticoats. Of course when I got there, I realised all the other girls were wearing crop tops and skirts in bizarre eight-year-old attempts to look like Kylie Minogue, and so I started to cry, asking to go home. She whisked me home, I changed my clothes and she took me back, with not one cross word about how long she spent on that stupid dress. I think I still have it in a box somewhere.

The lunch spread before us was a masterpiece.

We sat down and James was almost drooling. If I married him I'd have to buy in bulk, because I've seen that lad eat three hamburgers in a row . . .

My mother said, 'Dig in, kids!' I reached for a serving spoon, perhaps a little hastily because my mother's roast potatoes are to die for and I was planning to scoop at least six onto my plate before anyone noticed . . . when I realised that Vanessa and James were sitting very still.

'Go on', my dad said, smiling around the table, 'stretch or starve, we're not shy around here.' But Vanessa and James weren't about to stretch for anything – at least, not yet.

We hadn't said grace.

We never say grace at home. When I was a child my mother read a book called *The attitude of gratitude*. She went through a mad stage of grace-saying and made us hold hands around the table and sing, even in Pizza Hut. Someone actually stole our bread sticks while we had our eyes closed. We gave up after that. But not saying grace to Vanessa and James is the equivalent of blasphemy, worthy of a burning. It is NOT done.

'Let's say grace', I interjected, embarrassed.

'How lovely', my dad replied, obviously picking up on my distress. My dad's scary like that sometimes; he can read me like a book.

'Vanessa', Dad said quickly, 'why don't you say grace?'

Okay, maybe Dad reads me like a book with some pages ripped out. Vanessa saying grace is pretty epic, in the sense that the plague was epic; it lasted a long time, by the end you wished you were dead, and suddenly it answered that wish.

Vanessa gave thanks. This is what I remember, though I think I may have suppressed some of the worst bits in the inner dark rooms of my sub-conscious:

'Dear Lord. Thank you for what we are about to receive (at this point my parents think it is nearly over and start reaching for their forks) and thank you for this chicken, Lord, this chicken that nobly gave its life so that we might live. Thank you for these potatoes whose roots reached deep into your bounteous soil and also gave up their lives so that we might receive the glorious fruits of your overwhelming and constant grace (at this point my father's shoulders start shaking a little). We thank you for the fair hands of the wise mother who made this feast for our consumption (my mum made a face) and we thank you for the father who presides over this meal . . .

I pray you would bring blessing and victory into this house. In the name of Jesus, I call out the goodness and nourishment in this food and I pray that it would

– 64 –

course through our veins and anoint our organs before being expelled from our bodies (my father spluttered into a cough) and sent back to the ground from whence it came. In the name of Jesus I rebuke any disease or bacteria in this food and I pray that all dross would be burnt up with your righteous fire and sent back to the hell to which it belongs. In the name of the Father, the Son and the Holy Spirit, may he reside with us always. Amen.'

Everybody paused and we all waited with bated breath to see if she had actually finished, but she had her eyes closed and was mumbling something about being a warrior queen under her breath. At this point my mother, bless her, seemed to have had enough and practically poured sprouts into James's lap in an attempt to get things going.

Despite all that, the rest of the lunch actually went rather well. Plus the Lord may have spoken to me! I mentioned Hayley and the idea about the youth club. We chatted about it for a bit (Vanessa told everyone she felt that this youth club thought was nothing less than a dewdrop from the cloud above) and whilst I was munching my way through my fourth roast potato, my mother turned to me.

'You know, darling, sometimes I worry about you; you seem to do so much, what with your job and your church work and marathon training and everything. You do know it's not wrong to give something up, don't you? You don't have to do absolutely everything, dear.'

It was such a simple statement, but it *really* made me think. I do want to do something for those kids, but it's impossible for me to run a youth club with all my other commitments.

Perhaps it would be alright if I stopped doing something. And then my father piped up and said that he might know just the place where the kids could meet. He said there were a couple of disused rooms in the Civic Centre and although they weren't great, (apparently there was some problem with damp), it would be a start. He offered to make a phone call the very next day and see if he could book them for me. What an answer to prayer!

It's funny because I never thought that the answers would come from was my parents. I thought that someone in my church might have a connection, but here I was, right at home where I belonged and my father had the solution. Why do I think God only works in the church and on a Sunday morning?

When my dad described the room that could be used for the club, Vanessa shot me one of her smiley I-told-you-it-was-the-year-of-breakthrough-oh-ye-of-little-faith looks. James smiled too but looked a bit worried. I think he knows what I know – and that is if Mum's right and something has to go, then I have to give up my leadership role of my house group at church. It's the only thing that I can easily stop doing. I've already collected half of the sponsorship money for my marathon so I can't cancel that. I'm going to raise money for Stop the Traffik's Global Fund. And besides, I'm strangely beginning to enjoy all the running.

James was looking nervously across the table at me when Mum was giving me notice that I had stop doing something and his eyes seemed to be pleading with me: whatever you give up, please don't sacrifice the one thing that we get to do together. It's like he could read my mind. I think he actually loves me. I don't know whether anyone's been in love with me before, I think I sort of love him for loving me. But I don't know whether that's enough.

Note to self, must phone Nola and Robert and ask for advice.

Over dessert, I asked Dad to tell us about his new battle. James had this faraway look and didn't seem interested in listening, but Vanessa was all ears, as if it was absolutely vital that she, as the Lord's warrior queen, should hear this intelligence so that she could give my father the vital prayer support he needs and so ensure victory in the fight. She asked him loads of questions about it all, which I think pleased him.

Apparently it's more of the same incestuous corruption on the Council again. There is a big, old and rather grand building right in the middle of town, which the Council want to sell to a developer who has plans to develop an exclusive health spa in it.

The problem is that the developer happens to be a Councillor's wife's brother – the very Councillor who is leading the charge to get planning permission granted – and he hasn't declared an interest. And apparently his wife even owns half of the development business. It stinks. It's the beach hut debacle revisited.

Dad said that there isn't enough space for things as there is and that this building was supposed to be used for the community. He said it wouldn't cost loads of money to do it up a bit and it was disgraceful selling a building like that when our local library was the size of Harry Potter's cupboard.

But I'm worried for him. When he was fighting the battle of the beach huts, it took a lot out of him. He was passionate about his cause and yet he ended up losing almost everything.

I worry about his health.

*I pray, Lord, that you would do something about this spa thing.
I don't think I can have one more conversation about property
law, but more than that, I can't stand seeing my dad hurt and
under pressure. Thank you Lord for my parents, thank you
that they have always looked after me and I wasn't born to
some horrible half-wits like Hayley seems to have been. I pray
Hayley will find someone to look after her who is as nice as
my parents. And show me if it's right to give up the house
group. And if it is, help James to be okay with it. Amen*

## TUESDAY FEBRUARY 13th

I went to see Hayley again this morning. I received a police
report stating that over the course of last weekend, there was
some sort of 'domestic' going on at her aunt's and uncle's. I
rang the doorbell about eight times this morning but no-one
answered. I'm convinced I heard the TV though. However,
before I could be sure, I had to remove my ear quite sharpish
from the letterbox because something on the other side was
growling in it. They have one of those psycho dogs who seem
to think it's living in some post-apocalyptic nuclear winter,
where it must savage anything that comes along in order to
survive. I rang Hayley's school, but they didn't seem to know
who I was talking about. It seems that truancy is another issue
that I need to add to Hayley's case file.

*God, there must be something more I can do specifically for
Hayley? The youth club will be for all of the kids – but what
does Hayley need? Please protect her from those who wish to
harm her.*

I called Robert and Nola tonight to organise a chat about the house group leadership decision. We'll get together this coming Friday evening. I told Robert on the phone about the youth club idea and he said that it sounded very exciting. Robert has decided to tell the deacons (who are meeting tomorrow night) that I'm considering stepping aside from the group so that a replacement leader can be considered. He said that his doing that doesn't commit me either way.

## WEDNESDAY FEBRUARY 14th

### 6.30pm

I *did* get a Valentine's Day card and I'm not thrilled. It was a rather straight Christian card (I prefer the funny ones personally) with a picture of an ocean on the front and the words *Love and Blessings* in over-ornate gothic text inside. It was unsigned and all that was written was *'Always on my mind – with love.'* James doesn't disguise his writing very well. First I felt happy – it's always nice to receive a card; but then I felt bad because the card was from James. Then I felt even worse because I didn't even think to get him one. But then I realised that was stupid: sending him a card would be leading him on and that would be a bad idea.

I've read the bit in Leviticus 10 about Nadab and Abihu who were killed because they offered 'unauthorised fire to the Lord.' I am now a bit worried that my youth club idea might be just that – my own idea and not something from God – an unauthorised idea. Obviously, it's not that I fear being cremated and judged – I want to do the right thing. Realise that I don't have to be afraid, that I'm only trying to do

– 69 –

something for God and for the kids – but then I thought that perhaps what I'm really worried about is giving up the house group. And upsetting James.

Why is it that it's difficult to leave things? Christians are enthusiastic joiners, but not terribly good at being able to disconnect from anything. Certainly that's true when it comes to actually leaving a church. Years ago, before lovely Robert and Nola came to lead, a family got upset and decided to move on to another church. They were made to feel like fugitives from God, and yet that they were somehow surplus to requirements and that only the pure elect were sticking around, those with a sold out passion to the vision. Mr Hemming said very publicly at the time that the church is like a human body and that every healthy body needs a bowel movement. I couldn't believe my ears – suddenly these people who had walked in fellowship with us for years and who had given their time, talents and money very generously, were actually being tagged in that way. I thought of a few waste product analogies for Mr Hemming myself.

So I think that, despite these mad fears, I'm going to leave house group leadership. I haven't absolutely and definitely decided because I'd like to wait until Friday's chat with Robert and Nola, but that's the direction I'm heading towards. And they have been so understanding and supportive so far.

James won't be happy. I told him that that I was leaning towards leaving on the way home from the Sunday lunch at Mum and Dad's, and he went very, very quiet. After a ghastly long silence, he then tried to persuade me to carry on and said how much he enjoys co-leading the group with me and how well we work together, which I think is true. But I can't get this youth club issue out of my mind and I told him that I need him to help me in my decision. Vanessa, unusually, was very quiet as we drove back. Perhaps she was praying. Perhaps she wanted to let James and I have space to talk. In the end, James clammed up and folded his arms, making it clear that he didn't want to talk about it.

Oh, the other news is that the big fuss at Hayley's house turned out to be a fight over Hayley stealing her aunt's ciggies. Her aunt called me at the office this afternoon to ask if Hayley could have a fag allowance as well as the pocket money that she's provided with. She abruptly hung up when I said 'No.' I spoke to Hayley's school today as well – there was a mix-up because Hayley won't answer to her family surname at school and insists on being known simply as Hayley B. Hence the confusion in the register and an unfounded fear of truancy. At least the girl's getting an education.

### 10.55pm

Good house group tonight. We all did a catch-up, went round the circle and updated each other with our news and prayer requests. Nice. I didn't mention my thoughts about leaving – I'm still 1% wavering, especially tonight, because the group was so lovely and I'm still worried about James – even more so after the Valentine's card.

Over the obligatory cup of tea at the end of the evening, James came over and asked me if I'd got his card. I was a bit surprised that he was so forthcoming, especially as he hadn't signed it.

'I want to make it easier for you, Helen, so that you know exactly where things stand between us.' That freaked me out. Is he declaring love and that I'm *Always on his mind* because

I'm probably going to leave the group and this is a desperate stab at a romance with me? He's never asked me out before, but over the years we've known each other, his feelings for me have always been obvious, which has made it harder when I've not been able to return them. So now it looks like he's upping the stakes and moving in with a Valentine's Day declaration of undying love . . . yikes.

I got back to the flat (having gently turned down James's offer of a walk on the promenade) and called Vanessa. I was in a bit of a flap and needed to talk.

Her view is that James could be 'the one'. She asked endless questions about him – she's intrigued that he works so hard in the sound booth at church and she thought that it was great that he not only came looking for Hayley with us but waded into a gang of kids to ask if they'd seen her. He is a man with quiet authority, says Vanessa, he's practical, spiritual and faithful. She even went so far as to say that she's thankful that he's not put off by her weirdness, which is interesting, because it means that she's admitting that she can be weird at times.

So now I am confused.

*Lord, it's tangled fishing line time again. Please sort me out. Amen.*

### THURSDAY FEBRUARY 15th

Joy, joy, joy, a mystery has been solved and I got completely the wrong end of the proverbial stick. The postman arrived this morning bearing no less than five items of mail for me.

One was the electricity bill (a horrifically high winter bill – I must get out more and enjoy the benefits of other people's heating) and then there was an invitation to get one of those catalogues where you buy a pair of shoes and then spend the next twenty years paying for them at fifty pence a week and 1345% interest. The catalogue went straight into the recycling bin. But the other three letters were, in order of my opening them, (1) wonderful (2) wonderful and (3) hideous. Let's get to the wonderful ones first.

The first was a card – from James. It was an apology card, with the words *I'm so sorry* on the front and an amusing cartoon inside. But there was a long letter inside too, handwritten – and I realised that I'd been mistaken about the handwriting in the Valentine's card. James said that he wanted to apologise for his bad behaviour last Sunday. He said he couldn't believe that he'd sulked and then tried to talk me out of what I felt God was asking me to do. He told me that he completely respected my judgement on the matter and that, while the group would miss my leadership, he wanted me to know that he was fully supportive of my new venture. He said that, if I definitely decided to go ahead, that it would be great if our house group could have a little drinks and nibbles thing soon to send me off and thank me and also pray for the new work I'm doing. He even said that he'd be delighted to come along and help out if I'd like him to. He's such a whiz with computers and he's got a couple of older PCs which work perfectly well for games – he said we could set them up and also perhaps eventually have Internet access, if we could sort a connection. I think this is a great idea, although I'm a little worried about the Internet idea, as I don't want the youth of Frenton to be hanging out in my club and popping into naughty electronic chat rooms and asking each other what they're wearing.

Anyway . . . not only did James NOT send the Valentines Day card, but he's also cool with my leaving the house group. Hooray and hosanna! This was the card he was referring to at the group last night – now it all makes sense. It doesn't change or solve the fact that James obviously still likes and perhaps loves me, but at least he's not declaring it with passion or trying to make me stay in the group.

The next letter (still under the designation of 'wonderful') was a lovely card from the deacons, thanking me for my house group service and assuring me that they were praying for me as I considered leaving the group leadership and starting the youth club. Most of our deacons have the attitude that they want to catch people doing something right; they let people know that they're appreciated. I did notice one thing though – Mr Hemming didn't sign the card, which is unusual, simply because he's the senior deacon. Oh well. At first I thought that perhaps he wasn't at the meeting, because he had a cold, or was roaming Frenton promenade trying to catch young female runners out in their beguiling togs.

The third envelope contained (can you believe it?) an anonymous letter. It immediately revealed exactly why there was no signature from Mr Hemming on the 'Thank you' card from the deacons – he'd probably scurried off home to tell his gorgeous wife the news of what I was doing, which then led to the most poorly disguised anonymous letter in the history of unkind epistles. It read:

*Dear Helen*

*I am writing this letter to you anonymously as I think that it is best that you do not respond to me personally or even know my identity. Please prayerfully consider these words as being directly from the Lord and treat them seriously and not with fickle foolishness as the Israelites of old did (Ex. 32:1).*

*A little bird recently told me of your decision to abandon and wilfully cast aside your responsibilities as a house group leader in our church. I use this popular metaphor of a little bird telling me, of course, only figuratively as of course I do not converse with animals and the information came my way through a mutual time of sharing with a prayer partner (Eph. 6:19).*

*I understand that you are taking this step in order to focus on the development of some kind of youth club in the town. I was surprised, nay, horrified at this news and would like to ask you a number of questions, lovingly.*

*Have you reached this decision as a result of much prayer (Col. 4:3)?*

*Did you discuss your decision carefully with some of the elders of our church, therefore submitting yourself to their wise and manly authority (Eph. 5:21)?*

*Scriptures speaks of the hireling and good shepherd and the hireling who abandoneth his sheep when something more interesting takes his fancy (John 10:12). Is this perhaps the case with you? And anyway, do you know your heart and motivation in this, for great is the potential for self-deception?*

*Will this be a thoroughly Christian youth club, where only godly music is played? Will there be a clear and indeed sound epilogue opportunity at the end of each evening?*

*Will there be a selection of fine Christian literature, with excerpts from Scripture, taken from a reliable translation?*

*Search your heart, Helen,*

*Sincerely in Christ*
*From one who cares.*

*PS: God is love.*

I was relieved to hear from James, delighted to get the 'Thank you' note from the deacons and beside myself with anger at what is obviously a note from the Queen of tiresome, Mrs H. Was considering popping round to their home to commit an act of arson when another more pressing thought landed in my head. And that was this – if James didn't send me the Valentine's card . . .

. . . then who did?

## FRIDAY FEBRUARY 16th

**Late evening**

I think that Robert and Nola are possibly the most wonderful Christian leaders in the world and we're very lucky to have them in our church, if there's such a thing as luck. I took the thinly disguised epistle of venom from Mrs Hemming round so that they could take a look – and I thought Nola was going to pop round to the Hemmings and sort them out there and then. Nola is so quiet, so reasonable and yet there are times when she gets very angry when she sees religious people doing horrible things, like sending anonymous letters. She became so incensed and animated that Robert smiled and let her talk it all through with me.

She told me how she was so excited about the youth club – as a lecturer at the community college she often see kids dropping out of school and she thinks that a gathering point for kids is long overdue.

She also told me not to be intimidated by Mrs Hemming's notelet of death. Nola says that too many Christians have a messed-up notion that 'serving the Lord' is only about working in the church, as if God is a localised Deity who lives in the church car park. God loves his church, Nola says and we need to partner with him to see the church's ministries resourced – but most of all he is building his Kingdom.

'God's out there in the big bad world, Helen and he's doing his stuff and wants us to get involved. When we care, serve, listen, help out, or surprise people with kindness – the equivalent of the biblical cup of cold water given in Jesus' name – then the Kingdom is built and extended.'

And then Robert chimed in, very helpfully.

"Evangelism is important, Helen. But not everything that we do has to be overtly evangelistic. You don't have to have an epilogue, tracts and Christian music in order to make something that honours and pleases God. In fact, all of that might be thoroughly off-putting and not the purpose of the club at all. The Kingdom of God was the main emphasis of Jesus' teaching – and when we see life being done God's way, where people on the margins suddenly matter, where those who have been stereotyped suddenly find a welcome and where conversation and community can take place – then God is pleased. Go for it Helen – we're totally with you . . . '

Robert then said that he was going to have a word with Mr and Mrs Hemming. Apparently Mr Hemming *had* been in the meeting when my resignation from the house group was announced and he'd sported a face like thunder and then refused to sign the card. Now, with his wife joining in the mad trend to not provide a signature, things had gone way too far. And of course there's a certain irony about their being so uptight about this – and that is that they left our house group and don't attend one at all these days. Mrs Hemming is apparently of the opinion that they are too mature for the kind of trivial sharing that goes on in house groups, which is complete piffle. Anyway, Robert says that it's time for the Hemmings to know that this behaviour has to stop. Robert was going to have a chat with them. Nola smilingly offered to stop by with an incendiary device for them.

At the end of our chat, Robert said that anonymous letters had been a thorn in a lot of people's sides. Apparently D. L Moody, the über-famous evangelist, was preaching one time when someone decided to send him a vitriolic unsigned note while he was preaching. The nasty little message was passed across the pews to an usher, who took the folded note to the pulpit and placed it before Mr Moody. When he opened the note, Moody found that it had only one word written on it: 'Fool.'

'I've just had the oddest note,' Mr Moody said to the congregation. 'I often get letters where people write the letter but then forget to write their signature – but in this case, the person forgot to write the letter and just signed their name.'

I like D L Moody. I love Robert and Nola. I'd love to know who sent me that Valentine's card. And now I've made my decision. I'm definitely leaving the house group.

Managed eight miles today – the training is going well . . .

I feel so much better now I've finally made a decision to move on from leading the group. It does seem to me that Christians sometimes over-complicate decision making. Sometimes you have to make a decision and trust that God will sort it out, as opposed to spending so long waiting for a booming voice from heaven that nothing gets done. Katy is going to help James with leading the group, so a replacement for me has been found already. I'm still waiting to hear from Dad about the room for the youth club though.

Laura and I went out to a bar tonight with some other people from work. Boy, that girl can drink, but she holds it well. She was on her fourth vodka and lemonade before I had even arrived. As we sat there, I realised that my friends are so different. The thought of Vanessa and Laura actually ever having a conversation or even being in the same room fills me with dread. They are simply from different planets. And yet both have strengths in different ways. Laura is a survivor. And she's got an uncomplicated straightforwardness about life that's refreshing. Sometimes when I get into the paralysis of analysis, she'll come up with a blunt stun grenade sentence like: 'Oh, get over it.'

Her uncomplicated approach to life means that, every now and then, she'll make a statement so wise and yet so stupidly obvious. I was bold enough to confide in her the other day that I do feel guilty quite easily. Her response was as obvious as Mrs Hemming's bottom in lycra, but it stopped me in my tracks.

'Look, Helen, this Christian stuff you're into is about forgiveness, right?'

I agreed that this was very much a part of the Christian gospel.

'So, if you've messed up, sort it with your God and then move on. If you're going to believe that stuff, you might as well believe it all, including the good bits.'

And yet Laura does have a very obvious blind spot. She's having relationship problems with some creep called Dave. Apparently he's all 'intimate' with her in private but ignores her in front of her friends. It doesn't sound like he likes her much, but she seems smitten. I told her to ignore him for a bit, because I'm sure that's what you're supposed to do in that situation, not that I've had much practice. The funny thing is that, even though he's treating her badly, I'm kind of jealous. Maybe if I don't compromise, I'll never find anybody?

Why is it that Laura seems so full of common sense, but when it comes to Dave the dirt bag, she can't see that he's using her?

And why is it that, when it comes to life, I have so many questions?

*Lord, I pray for my future husband, I pray that'll you'll keep him safe for me and keep the nasty roaming hands of other women OFF him. I pray that he'll be completely and utterly in love with you, like I am. I love you. Night, night.*

## SUNDAY FEBRUARY 25th

Horrors. It's been ages since I've had a time of journal tapping. Mad at work.

Church this morning was great – one of those mornings where everything seemed to be perfect – almost. Robert's sermon on

'Becoming a servant' was excellent, not least because he acts like one, so happens to be a walking, talking illustration. Kristian did well with the worship – it was sane, accessible and inspirational and he kept to the allotted time. I smiled at him when he sat down. He smiled back, those baby blues flashing. Not only that, but I noticed that during Robert's sermon, Kristian was nodding and definitely taking notes – no song-writing for him today. Perhaps I've been too harsh with Kristian. We need to give each other room to grow.

Still no news from Dad about the room for the club.

Tonight Nola invited me round for a glass of wine and I found myself in the unusual position of having to cheer her up – which is odd, because it's nearly always the other way around. She's so discouraged. Apparently, Nola said that Robert went to have a chat with the Hemmings this afternoon and it didn't go well – actually all hell broke out. Robert began their meeting by thanking them both for their years of service in the church – he's so good at trying to bring the positive – but then mentioned the letter I'd received. Robert said that people who write letters should have the courage to sign them and that the church leadership should either totally get behind efforts to impact the community, or at least disagree with grace and kindness. At this point Mrs Hemming exploded. I've never seen *The Exorcist* film, but I can imagine that, if Mrs Hemming was 55 years younger and five stone lighter, she could do an outstanding head-revolving/bile spitting/ fingernails-growing-six inches-in-three-seconds act to produce a devil worshipper.

At first she even denied sending the letter until, in the end, her husband blew her cover by saying that he agreed with what his wife had written, which was unfortunate. Apparently she shot him a look that suggests that he is going to suffer when they're next alone. That man is probably never ever going to experience carnal relations again. Gross, I just had to pixalate my mind at the thought.

But then, perhaps that serves him right, because I've now come up with a word that best describes this lovely pair. Bullies. That's what they are – Bible-toting bullies who get their own way with a subtle violence that might actually be uglier than a punch in the mouth.

One of their weapons is the catch-all that I mentioned earlier. If someone does something that they don't like or would not be their personal choice, they can attack that person, not by using Scripture to justify their arguments but by simply playing the you-make-me-stumble card. And when they do quote the Bible, they simply seem to bruise people but not shed any light on their issues.

Then there's the unity/division/rebellion cards that they use. If anyone disagrees with Mr Hemming's leadership (or perhaps the real leader is Mrs Hemming who uses her husband like a puppet to get her way – even though she doesn't believe in women being in leadership), then Mr Hemming cries foul by saying that the person who disagrees is threatening the unity of the church with their 'divisive' comments. You can't ask them a question and anyone who tries to challenge them is tagged as being rebellious. No, they're not being rebellious; they've just got a brain cell and would like to use it.

Once Mrs Hemming admitted that she'd written the letter, (without apologising for lying) she then blustered on about how her words were hard, like Jesus' to the Pharisees and Paul's to the Corinthians, but they had to be spoken. She isn't responsible for God's standards, she said, and she was worried that the good name of the church might be smeared if it got out that someone from the fellowship (me) was running a youth club that was not absolutely Christ-centred. She ended the meeting by switching tactics and turning on Robert. It was his lack of sound teaching from a proper translation of the Bible that had helped create all this chaos. And then she played the ultimate hand: she said that he, the leader of the church, wasn't deep enough and neither were his sermons, what with all those silly little anecdotes and humour. Why, Jesus didn't laugh, did he?

The meeting ended up with the Hemmings virtually kicking Robert out of their house – but they didn't threaten to leave the church (which would have probably given rise to the throwing of an instant street party). Instead, Mrs Hemming yelled that there were not alone in their concerns, *that a good number of folk in the church were troubled.* And then the knock-out punch. They said that Robert should seriously pray about his future ministry at New Wave. The message was obvious. 'We're not leaving and you might be. We can make it happen. We were here before you came and we'll be here after you've gone. This church is ours. Back off.'

Nola actually cried when she talked about it. The Hemmings are bullies.

I realised as I passed Nola a Kleenex that I wanted to hurt the Hemmings. And then I realised that, in rightly calling them bullies, I could resort to bullying tactics myself. Nevertheless, they are wrong. God help me to keep my attitude clean and avoid ending up like them.

Do I love the Hemmings? No. Am I willing to love them? I'm not sure. Do I feel like loving them? No.

The great news is that I got a phone call from Dad – he's got the room and we can use it for a year at a peppercorn rent. He said again that the room's not much to look at, but it's a start. James is willing to lug the computers in and help with setting things up, so I think we're on a roll. Dad also said that the battle with the Council over the proposed sale of the proposed spa building – it's called Lawrence House – is hotting up – he's trying to get a public meeting organised. Said I'd pray for him, which I certainly will.

Loads of work to do now on setting the youth club up.

Saw Hayley, who was much the same and suggested that I might like to shove my head where the sun doesn't shine, which at first I thought was a reference to Alaska during the long winter months. Laura advised me differently.

A wonderful thing has happened – what with the news yesterday from Dad about the room for the youth club, today's terrific happening is turning this week into a fabulous time of almost apocalyptic proportions (not sure this is the best analogy, but it certainly is a good week!)

Stand by and hold onto something solid because the news is that *Kristian Vivian Rogers*, worship leader and love god of this parish, called me today and asked me out! Yes, I kid you not – but there's more . . .

He ever so casually asked me on the phone if I'd got the card.

My brain fogged over a bit and then I realised that he was the one who sent the Valentine's card! (I did ask him outright about it, in order to avoid any further confusion). I told him that I had no idea because the card didn't seem to be a style that I would have thought was his taste and he said that he'd been rushing around that day and had dashed into the Christian bookshop and grabbed the first Valentine's Day card he could find, off the shelf. This ever-so-slightly niggled me but I managed to stifle this because I AM GOING OUT WITH KV NEXT SATURDAY FOR COFFEE! Vanessa is right. This is a year of breakthrough.

Popped into the Civic Centre to see the room Dad has got for the youth club – and he's right, it's not much, but we should be able to put a pool table and a table tennis table in and a few tables with computer games, courtesy of James. Add a few music DVDs and at least we're off to a start.

## WEDNESDAY FEBRUARY 28th

It was such a lovely, lovely evening at the house group tonight. People said some nice things to me – I am far too embarrassed (and humble) to write them down here. Why is it that I am so good at taking criticism to heart, but struggle when people say nice things about me? One after another people took turns to thank me and say what my leadership has done to help them and then they prayed for me and the youth club, which was fantastic, although I did have one tiny niggly thought about that when I got home – more about that in moment.

Then James announced that the group had decided to take a little offering to help the club on its way – and they gave me an envelope with £679.27 in it! I am so excited. In fact, far more than I've raised so far for the marathon.

Back to my niggle (why do these weird thoughts come to me?) which is about the way that we do prayer. You see, we spent about thirty minutes in the group talking about the club – people asked me questions and I tried to explain as best I could what I felt we wanted to achieve – and we then spent the next twenty-five minutes telling God all the things that he'd heard us spend the first thirty minutes talking about. I know that prayer matters – and the prayers tonight came from people who not only love me but put their hands in their pockets as well – but I'm not sure that we always get prayer right.

I didn't tell James about my upcoming date with Kristian. I'm sure he'd be fine but I didn't feel totally comfortable with it. Will do so soon.

## FRIDAY MARCH 2nd

My sunshiny blue sky day was marred a bit because I had a confusing lunch with mad Vanessa today and we actually had a bit of a mild row – the first disagreement we've had in absolutely ages. I told her about my date with destiny tomorrow, hoping that she'd be thrilled for me, but she was the opposite.

Anyway, all her church-hopping means that she's only seen Kristian in action leading worship at our church once and she wasn't impressed. She said there was a subtle difference between worship leading and performance and that she felt that Kristian was a bit too impressed with himself. She was worried, she said, because after the service he was holding court with some of the younger girls in the youth group, while everyone else in leadership was praying with people at the front. She said she didn't feel a peace about me getting together with Kristian. Don't know what to think and I think I defended Kris with a little too much fervour. What that means is that I was close to yelling at Vanessa and telling her that I didn't care what she had peace about.

I'm hoping that Vanessa is wrong. But then she confused me by insisting that God only has one person alive on planet Earth that is chosen to be my partner and that I must not miss the best or compromise. Thinking about that for a bit tonight, I can't see how that works. For one thing, I can't find anywhere in the Bible that says that there's only one person you can marry. And then, what if you marry someone and they die and you marry someone else – was the second person being held as first reserve until the other one died? There seem to be some good biblical reasons why a divorce sometimes happens – so what if you have a biblical divorce and then you marry someone else – are they a reserve candidate too? Didn't come to any final conclusions, but decided once again that I must be willing to question some of the ideas that we Christians pass around to each other without thinking them through first.

Anyway, none of this is going to spoil tomorrow. Oh happy day to come.

## SATURDAY MARCH 3rd

Woe and thrice woe. Kristian and I met in the new coffee shop in the High Street and right from the beginning I knew that things weren't going well. For a start, he was late – thirty minutes late in fact. He didn't even apologise about keeping me waiting, but mumbled something about 'getting lost in God's presence as I was composing this morning.' Then, when we got coffees, not only did he let me pay for both of them, but he didn't even say 'Thank you' and made some snide remark about fair trade coffee being a big waste of time. I started to reply but he didn't seem to be interested in listening. And then, without asking anything about me, how my day had gone or anything, he launched into a long boring description of his morning. Apparently he likes to take every Saturday morning out to pray and compose. I sat there wondering why this man had sent me a card telling me that I was on his mind. He didn't seem to have room there for anyone else, apart from himself.

Anyway, I digress. According to delayed and fair trade despising Kristian, the Lord and he have cosy little chats when he spends time in solitude and picks up his guitar. Apparently a guitar is a conduit for some sort of special holiness. And then, incredibly, he said something like:

'Hel, I was writing this worship song this morning, ya know, getting into God's presence and I had this image of rushing water, you know, powerful but cleansing. And I felt that God was telling me to write a song about it, it was like he put the lines straight into my heart, and I wondered what you would think about it, Hel . . . '

He then launched into a very unattractive speech about how he wanted my 'input' because he had felt not only a strong spiritual connection with me but also that I was beautiful. That made me feel a little better – for about a minute. He also said that he was not consulting with the beaming worship backing singers, because he didn't feel the same connection with them in the Spirit. I was flattered at first and then managed to engage brain and decided that I didn't like the way this little chat was going at all. But then Kristian rounded up his monologue by launching into an arrogant tirade about what he calls 'yesterday's worship leaders'.

He said that he was one of the fresh voices that God was raising up, with a new DNA to connect totally with the angst in today's culture, and that many of the more established worship leaders were 'yesterday's people' who were 'tired, old hat and should make way for the new thing that God was doing. What is needed are real pioneers', he said, 'who will take risks.' I couldn't help thinking that some of those veteran songwriters and worship leaders had taken huge risky steps in their lives in a church culture that had been far less open to change than church is these days and that Kristian was lobbing a bunch of real pioneers into a skip. But I kept quiet, mainly because I couldn't get a word in. Then it got worse, because Kristian shared the words of the song that he and God had written this morning. Here's a brief excerpt as best as I can remember it:

'Rushing water flow, flow,
I am so lowly,
Love me slowly,
Jesus. Jesus. Jesus.
Let your gentle water-wings cover me,
Engulf me worshipfully.
Jesus. Jesus. Jesus.
You are the King-River of my heart.'

Groo!

I hope that he doesn't try to introduce it into our church, because one run through that little ditty and the entire congregation will be on a conference call with the Samaritans. Hopefully lovely Pastor Robert is far too sensible to allow Kristian to share this twaddle.

But then I realised that I had a big problem that I've bumped into before. How do you disagree with someone who claims that God has told them to do something, when it's obvious that he hasn't? If God gave Kristian that song, it was probably because God didn't want it in the first place. But when someone prefaces everything with 'God told me' or 'The Lord spoke to me' then that's it – discussion over. It reminds me of a conference that I went to last December on prophecy. Someone stood in the last service and loudly declared, 'Thus says the Lord of hosts, a very happy Christmas to all my people.' It was obviously mad – but they'd already decided that God was telling them to do this. Is 'God told me' sometimes a term that insecure people use to cover their tracks – or even a way to manipulate others into agreeing with them?

At the same conference, someone else 'felt' the urge to spontaneously lead the gathered congregation in a song and launched into *He'll be coming round the mountain when he comes*. This all went swimmingly until we got to the 'singing I, I, ippy ippy, I' bit, whereupon it died a fast death.

I do have a real problem with Kristian, because I'm starting to think that he's a bit of a pompous, self-obsessed drip, but I do fancy him. His musical drivel is unattractive and off-putting, but those blue eyes and blond hair and even now fading slightly tan are still very nice indeed. I'm confused.

That's it. I fancy him a lot and don't like him today at all. Vanessa was right.

I've only read four chapters this week, all from Jonah. I've always thought the story was about a large fish, and ever since watching *Veggie Tales*, I can't read this story without thinking of Jonah as a prophetic asparagus. But I was struck by how furious that little vege . . . I mean prophet got with God. He was in a real hissy fit and told God so. I wondered about some of my polite, speech-like prayers – some of which perhaps contain lies if I don't tell God what I feel.

Okay God. What I am about to say may give the impression that I am a very bad Christian. But reading Jonah has taught me that it's a good idea to tell you what's on my mind. I don't want to be judgemental, but it's hard enough to get people to believe in you without people like Mr Hemming sticking terrifying leaflets about hell in people's faces. During church this morning Robert was reading out the usual church notices: *Would anyone like to volunteer for church cleaning, the worship practice is on Tuesday nights, would people please ask for permission before they stick anything up on the notice board* . . . (Robert rather pointedly looked at Mrs Hemming when he mentioned the notice board, which I suspect might be a reference to the leaflet advertising a conference called *The King James: the Bible Paul used* that was pinned up anonymously).

To be honest, I wasn't concentrating. I was actually pondering the vital issue of what colour mine and Kristian's children's hair would be. My biology is strictly Key Stage One and I was trying to remember about recessive and dominant genes. Since I have dirty blonde hair and he has blond hair, there is a good chance we would have lots of beautiful blond-haired cherubs who might look mildly Swedish despite hailing from Frenton. And they'd tan beautifully. How cute would that be?

Obviously I have decided to forgive Kristian for his idiotic self-obsessed behaviour during that disastrous date. Time heals, it's been a whole 8 days since it happened and he did look utterly gorgeous this morning. Not only that, but he didn't try to teach his *King River* song to the church, which gives him points in my book. If he asks me out again, I will ponder, say that I'll need to think and pray about it, so will let him know in a day or two . . . and then will magnanimously say 'Yes' . . .

Anyway, I digress. At the end of the announcements, Robert asked if anyone had any other notices. Mr Hemming took that as an invitation to stride up to the pulpit and tell Robert that he needed to pass on 'a message from the Lord' to the congregation, which hardly constitutes a notice. Poor Robert's face was a picture, but before he could protest Mr Hemming grabbed the mike and was off. He launched into an impassioned rant about how God had called us all to be evangelists and we needed to take our responsibilities more seriously and that he was already leading the way by standing outside the local Tesco's on Saturdays, handing out booklets to passers-by. He was waving one around while he talked and it had flames on the front. FLAMES! And not only flames, but I'm sure I saw a little picture of a devil with a pitchfork as well . . .

Something tells me that this booklet isn't awash with good news. If anyone asks me why I'm a Christian, hell is the last issue I would think to talk about. I'm a Christian because of Jesus, not Satan. Why tell people about hell when you can tell them about heaven? Am I wrong? I don't know . . . another thing to talk through with Nola . . .

Anyway, apparently Mr Hemming's 'winning' technique is to point his finger at poor unsuspecting shoppers and bellow

'YOU ARE LOST AND YOU ARE GOING TO THE ABYSS!' in their faces. He finally finished his angry 'invitation' to others to come and join him for the Saturday morning evangelistic mugging. Strangely, he didn't have any stories about anyone actually converting. He did say that the devil did try to stop his good work by possessing a homeless man, who kept asking him for change. But apparently he rebuked him in the name of Jesus and the man wandered off. Sometimes I think Mr Hemming doesn't get it, but then I think, if Mr Hemming doesn't get it, maybe I don't get it either, seeing as I don't think I've converted one single person in my whole Christian life, nor has anyone ever got better when I've prayed for them, at least from any epic illnesses. I've prayed when people had coughs and colds, but never knew if they recovered quickly because (a) the cold ran its course (b) they nuked it with Lemsip or (c) a congestion-battling angel of the Lord was despatched because of my intercessory efforts. Option (c) doesn't seem that likely.

Last year I prayed loads for Mrs Malone who was dying of cancer and I believed she would be alright. But she still died. Perhaps I don't believe in God enough. But how can you tell, it's not like you can measure faith with a meter, can you? And how does that work out with God anyway? When he heard my prayer, did he say, 'Mmm. Helen has 91.45% faith but in order to spare Mrs Malone from a painful death Helen needs to get that faith level up to a minimum of 96.34% . . . sorry Mrs M, it's time for you to get hooked up to the morphine drip and prepare yourself for a painful demise . . . '

I must ask Nola about all of this.

*Lord, please help my unbelief.*

I'm confused about the heaven and hell and healing and faith thing. In fact I'm confused about lots of things. But I *am* certain I don't want to adopt Mr Hemming's techniques. I've decided that Mr Hemming might be like Jonah, who preached loudly but hated the people he preached to. And I'm not sure that it's a good idea to call people 'lost'. They *are* lost if they don't know God, but surely that's not the end of the story, is it? The fact that God sent Jonah hot-footing it to wicked Nineveh means that he is desperate to *find* people – he's the good shepherd who goes hunting for his idiotically wayward sheep. So perhaps a better term to describe people who don't know God is *sought*, not *lost*, because there's a God who urgently wants them to know his love . . .

All this threatens to make my head explode. Okay, some good news: Robert told me after the service that the deacons had voted to buy a pool table for the youth club (not unanimously – there was one vote against, surprise, surprise) so things are coming together well. We're still a way off from being able to open, though. Once we start, I want us to be open consistently, every Friday night for starters, so I've decided to wait until after we get back from our annual Easter church trip to Together for the Kingdom, a big Christian bash that they hold in the north. We've got a group of about sixty going and Robert and Nola are coming too, which is lovely. I'm so glad I can call them my friends. Our last minister had told everybody that he would be 'shepherd of all and friend to none', because during his training he'd been taught to have no favourites. But Robert has made it clear in his teaching that we all need friends and he wouldn't live under that kind of prohibition. Robert and Nola are both very wise – strangely, they're a little like Laura, but Robert and Nola know where their wisdom is coming from. It's more than common sense.

They know God and they know their Bibles. And they're kind and ordinary and all round nice human beings that I'd like to be like. Roll on Easter.


## TUESDAY MARCH 13th

Laura at work had the distinct misfortune to pop into Tesco's for a loaf of bread last Saturday and told me that she'd met a very odd man and asked me if he was from my church. I coughed and mumbled something about not being sure if he was – which is terrible! I denied even knowing Mr Hemming, which is a lie . . .


## SUNDAY MARCH 18th

**Lunchtime**

I can't believe another whole week has gone by. I've been working hard on my running, which is going well. I had a nice coffee catch-up with Vanessa last Wednesday and she told me that they are having a special interdenominational healing service at Infusion tonight, so I'm going along.

Church was good again this morning. Robert spoke on the power of love from 1 Corinthians 13 and said that the famous chapter was far more than good material for fridge magnets. Kristian led worship well. I'm glad I decided to give him another chance last week, seeing as Jesus has given me about a billion other chances, but Kris still hasn't asked me out again. I tried to catch his eye a couple of times this morning, but without success.

After the service I told James about the healing thingy at Infusion and he's planning to come and bring the house group too. He said that Kristian found out about it and had asked if he could tag along with us, which James didn't seem too thrilled about. He said that the outing was an opportunity for our house group to bond a little and as Kristian is not in the group, that it wasn't a good idea. Then he said that despite this he didn't feel like saying 'No' to Kristian, which I was glad about because I felt quite excited about spending some time with him again. I also thought that James has forgotten that I'm no longer in the house group, so the bonding argument doesn't wash . . .

Anyway, I'm glad that Kristian is coming. Perhaps he had been horribly embarrassed about that appalling date and has been trying to summon up courage to ask me out again. *Grant him boldness, O Lord* . . .

### Just before bed

My, what a night. I met Vanessa outside the school that Infusion rents for their meetings. She was carrying a 'prophetic sculpture' that she'd made for the evening. She said that it represented the leaves for the healing of the nations.

There was a guest speaker – a rather odd evangelist chap with very strange hair who is planning to come back to Frenton later in the year to hold what he called a 'crusade.' Wondered if this involved people dressing up as medieval warriors and then galloping along the promenade in search of heathen to convert, impale, or both. Mr Hemming would like that . . .

The service, to be honest, was awful. Got the distinct impression that God was in dire need of persuasion to heal, seeing as this evangelist prayed at an ear-splitting volume.

People who were prayed for were asked to immediately declare that they were healed, which was both embarrassing and heartbreaking. Weird-hair shoved a microphone in the face of a girl who'd asked for prayer for a stutter and gleefully announced that she'd be able to speak perfectly. Cue loud applause and cheering from the congregation. All went rather well, at least for a few words. Then she said, 'I'm really grateful that Je-Je-Je-Je-Jesus has he-he-he-healed me', which is when the clapping stopped. I wanted to cry for her.

Then Doris, a lady from our church who is hard of hearing, was asked to repeat what the evangelist was whispering in her ears as proof that she was now sorted. 'Jesus is Lord!' he muttered into her left ear and the microphone, so that we'd all hear what he said. 'What did I just say to you?' he asked, an eager grin all over his face.

'O God, I'm bored', she said, with feeling.

Then the fiasco got worse. A chap with something wrong with his knees was prayed for and then he was told to run up and down the platform. This he did without too much hobbling, which prompted more clapping, though it was more nervous applause this time. Thrilled that he'd finally got something close to a result, the evangelist demanded that the chap with the healed knees do a victory lap around the hall. He dutifully obliged, but unfortunately got excited as he came steaming up the centre aisle like a bat out of he . . . heaven. Sadly he didn't notice Doris's handbag, left in the aisle. He tripped, went flying and broke his ankle, becoming perhaps the first person to be taken to casualty *from* a healing meeting.

It was during the singing of the last song that the most embarrassing event in the history of the Universe happened.

I noticed that Doris's handbag had been kicked onto the platform by the sprinter with the knees and she needed her glasses to be able to see the song words on the screen. Because she couldn't see the words, she was singing 'la,la,la,la,la' at the top of her voice like an elderly out-of-tune Teletubby. I thought I'd retrieve her bag for her, but I hadn't noticed that the wooden floor had been liberally splattered with the olive oil that the evangelist had used for the praying. There's a certain naughty word that automatically comes out of my mouth whenever I'm hurt, shocked or scared, and as I skidded and slid my way across the greasy floor, I screamed this word without thinking. I then smashed into Vanessa's prophetic tree and the leaves for the healing of the nations were scattered all over the platform, like it was suddenly autumn.

Finally I found myself face down on the floor looking like I was prostrating myself in worship before Mr Evangelist Weirdhair – but then a certain sense of discomfort confirmed to me that, in the tumble, my scarlet red thong had ridden right up my back and was now on full display to everyone. I staggered to my feet, conscious that a few people in the crowd were giggling and one or two actually stuffing Bibles into their mouths . . . James rushed forward to help me up, but then as I turned around, I noticed that Kristian was giggling too and he had this rather stupid leer on his face.

I am starting not to like him again now. I punctuate a Christian gathering with a yelled expletive and then flash my underwear at everyone and he thought it was funny. Not nice.

At last the service ended, we cleaned up the oily tree branches, had a terrible cup of tea and headed for home. We gave Kristian a lift and he talked endlessly about how he'd had prophecies that he was going to take his music to the nations of the earth, that he frankly felt more at home in the large setting of Infusion tonight, and that he was born to lead huge crowds in worship. He also ripped into the poor lady who led the songs, because she had us sing a couple of older worship songs and even a hymn. I couldn't help thinking about poor deaf Doris who was sobbing her way through *Amazing Grace.* Her deafness means that she yells everything and over the appalling cup of tea I overheard her bellowing that she'd sung that hymn on her wedding day and at her husband's funeral, so it meant a lot to her. I was wrestling with the temptation to break Kristian's guitar (he calls it his harp) over his head (he'd taken it with him tonight, even though he wasn't leading worship, because he says it's an emblem of his God-given identity). The more he went on, the more I wanted to hurt him. But then, bizarrely, I'd still like to kiss him as well. I am sick in the head . . .

Oh, nearly forgot. Mr and Mrs Hemming also showed up at the healing service tonight and she was ranting over the mud-coloured nasty tea about how she'd only attended the event because she was suspicious that unsound teaching was being proclaimed. As a 'watchperson of the Lord', as she described herself, she was gravely concerned because her worst suspicions had indeed been confirmed. My problem is that she is probably right – the evangelist chap taught that suffering comes when we don't exercise enough faith and that he avoids sickness because the Holy Spirit warns him that suffering is coming, like a heavenly air traffic controller. I'm no theologian, but I know that's tosh.

So what with the healings that were probably iffy and then the way Awful-hair murdered Scripture in his preaching, Mrs Hemming might be right . . . and yet, she's wrong. She may be correct and orthodox, but her attitude stinks. She was sniping at a greater volume than poor old deaf Doris, but she never once went up to the visiting evangelist who looked like he was praying over the dishwater tea to try to make it drinkable (without success, from the look on his face). I remembered Robert's sermon from this morning, when he said that if we don't speak the truth in love, then we don't speak the truth. Remembered too how Mr Hemming had loudly barked 'Amen' at that point in the sermon and then turned around and glowered at everyone in the church, as if to say, 'You lot need to hear this.' What about his acid-tongued spouse who was parked next to him?

Anyway, back to Mrs Hemming's 'Tonight's preacher was unsound' speech at the healing service. She got on a roll. James wandered over to her to say 'Hello', more to shut her up really. Small talk seemed the best way, but James said that Mrs Hemming continued her ear-splitting rant about the evangelist and the evening. He made his excuses and we fled.

So now, I'm off to bed and I feel a bit depressed. We Christians are supposed to love each other, but some are tough to even like. Kristian is not only more and more irritating, but also irritates me more because I'm still attracted to him. It's not his fault, but I feel like blaming him anyway. James is lovely and it was nice that he came to rescue me when my thong was almost wrapped around my earlobes, but there's still no spark. As for the Hemmings, words fail me. I wish that words would fail them.

I'm exhausted. Need sleep. Need faith. Goodnight.


## WEDNESDAY MARCH 21st

Truly a few days from hell. I started the week feeling a bit morose after the healing service debacle. Perhaps the only good thing about that disastrous evening is that it's unlikely that the evangelist is going to hit Frenton with a crusade now.

I had to go to see Hayley again yesterday and her dislike of me has now become more and more obvious. She hinted her irritation by opening the door and telling me to go forth to another place swiftly (won't write down what she actually said but I think I learned a couple of new swear words today). She then informed me that she hated my guts, she wished I'd get into a terrible and fatal car accident and be burned alive in the petrol-fuelled flames and that I'd done nothing to help her. I mentioned that I was doing my best, whereupon she said, very slowly, 'Well done' and then she actually gave me a slow hand clap. I'm quite good at my job and I'm normally confident enough, but I wanted to burst into tears. Bit my lip.

Lunch with Vanessa didn't go so well either. She didn't seem to be listening (and that's so unusual for her) when I told her about my desire to gag the Hemmings, and about Hayley and even that I wanted to punish Kristian a little for his smirking (but would end up kissing him better). She rattled on about how her prophetic tree had been shattered by my little oil-based trip, but how it was no accident. There are no coincidences, she says, just God-incidences. Everything therefore means something. But I can't get my head around that at all. God doesn't plan everything – and everything doesn't have a purpose, does it? Little children are abused and trafficked and God doesn't plan that, does he? Got exhausted thinking about it, so gave up. Looking forward to getting away to Together for the Kingdom.

Dad phoned and said that he'd managed to get a great deal on a brand new table-tennis table for the club, which he and Mum are going to donate. At least things are coming together in that area of my life. I'm planning to open on Friday April 27th, just over four weeks from now. Need to recruit some more helpers. Also need to do endless forms, checks, admin, etc etc, all of which is boring and time-consuming so am not going to waste more time by writing it about it here. I will be glad when it is all over!

## FRIDAY MARCH 23rd

The bad news is that I think I may just have been sexually assaulted by a Scottish terrier. It may have something to do with the fact that, because of all this exercise, I no longer resemble an over-stuffed sausage in my Lycra gear. I'm no chipolata but I definitely look better than I did before! I don't seem to be driving men blind with desire (still no invite to another date from Kristian) but I do seem to be having an alluring effect on small animals.

I was running in the park this morning, mumbling prayers under my breath. I began praying for my friend Laura's miraculous conversion but the prayer quickly turned into more of a gasping plea for God to please, gasp, make my lungs stop burning like a fire in a paper factory, when who should I smack right into but Kristian! Whilst grabbing onto him gasping and trying to apologise at the same time, I noticed that his eyes were all red, like he'd been crying.

I asked him what was wrong and we ended up sitting on a bench for forty minutes discussing his pain. Apparently things haven't been going too well for him, he'd been getting some vibes of criticism about his worship leading style and he was beginning to wonder whether New Wave Christian fellowship was the right place for him after all. I felt slightly put off by this, because I so love our church. He started talking about how he feels that God has given him all these dreams about influencing the whole world with his songs, but that no doors are opening and he feels trapped in the small backwater that is New Wave. I felt a mixture of sympathy and irritation about that, but then came the mad dog attack.

The assault came from Barnabas, Kristian's Scottish terrier. He's definitely a cute little thing (the dog, not Kristian. Well, and Kristian . . . ), but during the whole conversation, in which I was trying to pull that sympathetic and wise 'I am your friend, let me offer you profound and spiritual advice' face, Barnabas was (as Barry White would have put it), trying to make sweet love to both of my legs at the same time.

Kristian was so caught up in his own misery that he didn't seem to notice and I kept trying to shake the poor thing off without looking like I had some sort of problem. After a while, it all got a bit much, because Barnabas was going at me like a jackhammer. So, with a little more violence than I intended, I suddenly kicked my leg out, which flipped the dog up into the air (he did a rather impressive triple somersault) and then he landed sprawled and stunned on his front, yelping and whining like the rejected lover that he was.

Kristian gave me this appalled look as if I should immediately be arrested by the RSPCA for cruelty to animals. And then he asked if that was necessary and then he started to cry again. The poor man really does love his dog. I felt so bad that I offered to buy him coffee, on the condition that Barnabas was left outside. We went and actually had a good time and I managed to tell him about my youth club and Kristian offered to come in one day and lead worship.

I gave him a half-hearted reply, because I can't imagine some of the kids I know singing songs about rivers and mountains. I *can* imagine them stealing his guitar and giving him an education about some of the finer points of the songs of the rapper, Fiddy Threepac, whose most recent single was entitled *Head-stamping* . . . I still find Kristian irritating and attractive in almost equal measures.

Spoke to Mum on the phone tonight. She said Dad's been working flat out on fighting the spa proposal and that he's trying to pull a public meeting together so that people can air their views openly. I hope he wins this one.

## SATURDAY MARCH 24th

I've had the strangest day. I phoned James this morning and told him about how Kristian is discouraged and could use our prayers, but he didn't seem too concerned and made some comments about Kristian needing to live in the real world and get rid of some of his head-in-the-clouds ambition. James is usually very caring but he obviously isn't too keen on Kristian.

Then I went straight into town after my run along the beach, a run where I nearly surrendered both my ears to frostbite despite wearing the red woolly hat my grandmother knitted me when I was thirteen. I had decided to buy a book by this guru guy, Bshach Yabba, so I could engage in what I hoped would be an intelligent theological debate with my mother.

The hope is that I will say some incredibly profound things and she will realise she has made more than a few deeply illogical errors, tear out her crystal nose ring (though hopefully not too violently) and declare that Christ was the one true God. Then she will rebuke Bshach Yabba in the name of Jesus and sob on my lap, begging for forgiveness. This seems to be a running theme in my Christian fantasies.

I decided to go to a rather junky-looking bookshop down Penny Alley because it has a reputation for selling quirky books. I ducked in, careful to avoid my reflection in the shop window, as I'd rather not be reminded that my red hat was clashing beautifully with my bright pink face. Not too mention that my lycra jogging gear made me look like I was smuggling saddlebags and two small bags of flour. I might be thinner than I was, but am not yet thin enough and the eating lapses of this last week haven't helped.

The guy behind the counter was slouched in a chair, his legs propped up on a desk, his head immersed in a copy of *Thus Spoke Zarathrustra* – you know, that bizarre book written by Nietzsche who declared that God is dead. Anyway, I made a half-hearted attempt to try to find the *Chakras and Sacrifice* book, before I got bored staring at endless rows of book titles, which were called things like *Wearing Derrida's Mouth-guards – speaking before you're spoken to* as well as the surely riveting *Philosophy and the Abyss – transgressing the crevice? and* the potentially intriguing *God, the Dirty Dancer of Death.*

I decided to ask for help.

At first I tried to attract the attention of the shop assistant in the classic British way – where you stand still and occasionally glance nervously at the sales person. When that didn't work, I decided to move a bit closer and stare at him more fixedly, even clearing my throat and shuffling round a little. However, he was completely and utterly engrossed in his book. I tried to catch his eye but all I could see was a head of long chestnut curls and so I was finally forced to ask him for help.

'I would happily help you, madam', he replied, his head still buried in his book, 'but how do I know you actually exist? You might be a figment of my imagination, something dreamt up by my senses to play with my mind.' I paused, because, to be honest, I didn't know what to say to this. If I knew I was going to be forced to engage in philosophical debate, I'd at least have brushed my hair and put my reading glasses on. They make me feel more intelligent.

'Listen', I finally replied, 'could you help me find a book called *Chakras and Sacrifice* by Bshach Yabba?'

He still didn't look up. 'Absolutely not, because that book is a pile of guano. A waste of time. Trees were cut down needlessly to produce that useless book.'

With this he finally looked up and . . . guess who it was . . .

It was Aaron, my boyfriend from Uni days. He looked slightly different now with long hair (to be honest it suited him much more than that horribly boring crew cut he used to have at university), but it was him alright. He was wearing a black polo neck and black jeans, with those ridiculously long pointy shoes that are back in fashion, also in black – I think they're called Winklepickers.

'Hi Helen!' he exclaimed and then babbled a non-stop stream of questions and answers without pausing for breath.

'It's been ages. Why on earth are you trying to buy a book by Bshach Yabba? Have you given up on the Christian malarkey? Well, you won't find any answers there. I've looked.

All I got was a sprained back from all those positions that Yabba insists that you contort yourself into.'

I looked confused. Well, in fact my confused face is also my 'I've just had a disturbing thought' face, as I momentarily considered Aaron in a variety of contorted positions.

'You know, from the yoga,' he explained.

'Oh', I said, obviously looking relieved. 'No, the book isn't for me, it's for my mother, well, at least I'm reading it for my mother. She's got into the chakra thing, you see, and I wanted to find out what it's all about so I could help her.'

'Right. Still dancing the Christian fandango then, Helen? You were always so much better at it than I was. You were a natural, whereas I always felt like I didn't know what I was doing, like I didn't belong. I used to hand out all these leaflets and go to all these Christian events because I thought that's what Christians did, but it never made me feel like a Christian, or at least what I thought feeling like a Christian would feel like . . . '

I had absolutely no idea what to say. I mean, I hadn't seen the man for about a decade and here he was jumping right in and telling me his deep, spiritual problems within seconds of saying 'Hi.' In fact I'd just realised that I hadn't actually said 'Hi.' Plus, this was the man who had actually dumped me for not being holy enough. I managed a rather fake sounding 'Oh dear' which came out of my mouth and sounded like sarcasm, though I did mean it. I felt bad for him. But 'Oh dear' was the best I could manage. There was a long silence that felt like an hour.

'I like your hat', he suddenly blurted out and moved into another machine-gun monologue. 'It's very retro, makes you look like you're from the seventies, wow, I mean, I wish I could be in the seventies now. There seemed to be so much more energy back then.' (How would he know, I wondered? He wasn't born until 1980!) 'People seemed to care more about stuff. Have you been running or something, you look all pink. It's nice, healthy looking. I don't do much exercise any more. Sometimes I just lie in bed for days.'

He sighed, but he didn't just sigh, he sort of put his whole body into it, it felt like the sigh took about two minutes, during which I once again blurted out 'Oh dear.' Then I actually felt like I wanted to sigh too, but had to hold it in because I was worried that he might think I was taking the mick. Which to be honest, I was now seriously considering doing. I felt sad for his sadness but a bit bemused by the strange, odd bloke that he had become.

'Good book? I asked. Not that I cared, but I wanted to say something, anything to break the now incredibly awkward silence that was creeping between us. He didn't seem to hear my question but kept staring moodily into some middle distance. I had to keep stopping myself from turning round to see what he was looking at.

And then suddenly he spoke again. 'Do you like Nietzsche?'

'Ummmm, sure, I haven't really read much.' I blushed, this was not going well. He was the weirdo, so why did I suddenly feel like a class A idiot?

'It's good. Really good. You should read it. It's very poetic. But it's dark, it makes me shiver, you know, when I'm alone. But there's something very powerful about it. Very honest.'

'Oh', I said yet AGAIN. I am truly the world's number 1 thicko.

I felt like someone had removed my brain and replaced it with bits of carpet fluff. I wish I read more books. Nola's great like that. Her knowledge as a philosophy lecturer means that she would know exactly what to say in a situation like this. Instead, do you know what I did?

I panicked and asked him out for coffee. I asked Aaron Byrne out for coffee! I have no idea why I did it. It seemed to rise out of my sub-conscious like vertigo.

'I don't drink coffee these days', he replied. 'I drink gin.'

'Oh', I said again, 'that would be fine too.' I am a complete and utter moron. Mentally challenged mice have higher IQs than me. Anyway, the long and the short of it is that I am now committed to going for a drink next Saturday night with a man who not only DUMPED me, but who now also seems to be several sandwiches short of a picnic. In fact he seems to have replaced the picnic with a pack of menthol cigarettes, a bottle of gin and a mental problem. *God, how on earth do I get myself in these situations?*

Having asked the man who dumped me out for a drink, I turned and fled the shop. And I never did get that Yabba book. I went in there to try to help one mildly confused person – my mother. And now I've invited another massively confused person into my life, in the shape of Aaron. I'm now confused myself. But pleased, for some reason, because Aaron said 'Yes'.

## SUNDAY MARCH 25th

You can now call me Helen of Troy Sloane. Apparently, I am so fair and lovely that men everywhere are fighting over, okay let's face it, my slightly blotchy and covered-with-ink hand. My face could probably launch a thousand ships, full of men ready to fight for my favours . . .

Anyway, at church this evening we had a special worship service, which basically means you cut the sermon time in half and end up waving your hands about with a little more enthusiasm than usual. At some point I think you're suppose to cry or laugh and have a bona fide RELIGIOUS EXPERIENCE, perhaps one of the ones that makes you live up a pole in the desert, wearing nothing but a loin cloth and filth. Kristian was on stage per usual, white teeth gleaming in the special lights he had rigged up to make the evening more 'inviting' for the Holy Spirit.

Personally I think if the Holy Spirit decides to turn up somewhere, he doesn't give a flying doodah-dash about mood lighting. I hope not anyway, because he's the One who brings healing and hospital wards don't tend to have dimmer switches.

Anyway, Kristian was in the middle of this loooooooooooooong speech, which seemed to involve him saying a lot of things like 'We have to open ourselves fully up to God, caress his face and love him deeply like a lover', while at the same time playing E minor over and over again on the guitar.

*God, I'm not sure whether it's wrong to say this, but here goes . . . sometimes worship songs sound a bit, well, physical. I think it's weird to have a whole church singing things like 'I want to go deeper' or 'Engulf me with your warm love until I break.'*

*Lord, I know our relationship with you should be intimate, but the way these songs sound, sometimes I'm not sure*

*whether I'm supposed to follow you or snog you. I hope I'm*
*not saying anything really blasphemous?*

Maybe I feel like that because I have a horribly corrupt and perverse mind. But what happened to all the songs with an actual story? No-one ever seems to sing about characters from the Bible, no-one even seems to sing about the miracles Jesus did or the stories he told, but instead we go on endlessly about the fact that he loves us so much. Some songs don't even seem to have a clear narrative, they tend to say kind of blurry things about love and faith and rivers and then repeat them over and over again . . .

Anyway, Kristian was mid-sentence, when suddenly the sound started going funny. It was strange because the sound NEVER goes funny at church, which is pretty much due to the fact that James is in charge of it and when James is in charge of something, it never goes wrong. He's fantastic with anything electronic, it's like he has some sort of post-modern techno-gift from God.

So Kristian's speaking in that mildly hallucinogenic worship leader's voice and the PA starts shrieking and screaming and doing that thing that makes everybody violently clap their hands over their ears and yell because it makes their back teeth hurt. Kristian didn't know what to do, since the deafening feedback completely ruined the atmosphere he had been carefully creating for the last twenty minutes.

Kristian muttered something that no-one heard because by now the PA was off. He had a face like thunder as he ended his 'set', as he calls it. Robert got up to preach and handled the whole situation beautifully. Strangely, as soon as Robert took the microphone, the PA came back on again, minus the screaming. He said that often we only notice those who serve us technically when something goes wrong and so he had us all applaud our faithful sound engineer, James, who flushed bright red with embarrassment when everyone clapped.

After the service James came to me and quietly asked me to pray for him – I thought that perhaps he was mortified about the screaming banshees in the PA system. And then he confessed something terrible to me. He said that he was so sick and tired of Kristian and his prima donna attitude and his pretentious ambitions that he had deliberately cranked up the PA in order to hijack Kris's set. I was a little bit shocked, but a little bit delighted too. For once, dutiful, responsible James had done something risky. And I think he did it because he's jealous of Kristian and the fact that I like him. Okay, it was very naughty of him and he certainly shouldn't have disturbed the worship like that. But I laughed all the way home when I thought about him doing that and then getting a congregational round of applause for his faithful service thirty seconds later. Perhaps Vanessa is right. Perhaps he might be the one.

So now I have James getting edgy and naughty because he wants me and Aaron wants to drink gin with me and that means he wants me and Kristian is perhaps coming to his senses and is realising that he wants me too. Life is looking interesting . . .

## SATURDAY MARCH 31st

I've eaten virtually nothing all day, due to nervous energy expended about date with Aaron tonight which is mad because I'm not even sure this is a date and if it is I'm not sure that it should be or that I want it to be and I AM SO CONFUSED! Decided to go with the flow and enjoy the evening. Aaron is so totally mad it might be high in entertainment value.

### 6:05pm

We are going to a poetry and music night in a rather trendy café near his bookshop. It's not Covent Garden, but for Frenton, it's about as on-the-edge as it gets. Apparently poetry has changed Aaron's life. Poetry has also momentarily changed my life because I am now in a state of blind panic, as I'm unsure about what exactly one should wear to a poetry gig; a beret and a striped top perhaps? That might look like I'm taking the mick, but what if I turn up in something completely inappropriate and everyone realises that I'm just a boring Christian with absolutely no handle on the bohemian underbelly of Frenton? I shop in Gap, for goodness sake.

I managed to shave one leg before the razor broke, so that at least means skirts are out of the question – don't want Aaron to think that he's out on the town with the Yeti. I have found my top, drunk some wine, done my hair, drunk some more wine, and am wondering, why I am making such an effort, when it's not like I'm actually allowed to date this guy properly? He's practically a card-carrying atheist from the sounds of it.

### 7:30pm

*Lord, please help me to be stunningly profound tonight so that Aaron will instantly believe in you again. I mean, he did it once, how hard can it be?*

It is April Fools' Day and guess who is the fool . . .

Alcohol is clearly a weapon sent by Satan to destroy us all. As I mentioned, it's April Fools' Day and the joke is very much on me. As I tap away here, the mere sound of my fingers on the keyboard is sticking red-hot needles into my frontal lobes. My stomach feels like it has an urgent need to express itself and I don't know what I ate last night, but if it wasn't road kill, why do I have this strange furry taste in my mouth? Did I perhaps snack on a kitten? However, I must write this to try and get my feelings straight about last night. It was such a blur of emotions; I'm not sure exactly how to feel about it. What I do know is that I feel very, very bad: physically, emotionally *and* spiritually.

Let me put it plainly: last night's little outing with Aaron was a terrible idea. It pains me to remember the details . . . but remember I must.

I met Aaron at the café – I was about ten minutes late, what with the wine and everything. He didn't seem to mind but the poetry reading had already started so I had to sneak in quietly. As I tiptoed towards his table, I tripped, and the guy on the mike gave me a very pointed look and sarcastically thanked me for paying attention. Aaron stuck his tongue out at him, which made me giggle and I received another dirty look, which made Aaron make a vigorous movement with his right hand. He had already bought a bottle of wine although, since he produced it from his inside jacket pocket, it probably wasn't from the bar. He poured me some in a glass that I'm sure still had somebody else's dregs in and we sat back to watch and listen. Each act was only allowed on for ten minutes and even though some of them were awful, there were a couple that were actually alright. The MC was very funny and the audience kept heckling drunkenly in the background. Aaron either enthusiastically applauded or muttered *Philistine* under his breath and kept whispering rude things about the performers in my ear. I never realised that he could be so funny. It made me think that maybe we should heckle in church a bit more, it might liven things up, but then I thought about what would happen if Mr and Mrs Hemming were allowed to heckle.

Aaron seemed to be drinking a lot and during the interval he produced another bottle of wine from somewhere and opened that too. After the interval was over, we went back inside, (we went out so that Aaron could smoke a bizarre brown roll-up he had which he said was liquorice flavoured). But we'd spent so long chatting, by the time we got back in, there was only one chair left. I went to offer it to Aaron, obviously keen to show him that Christians aren't all bad and some actually offer their seats up for others, when he sat down on it and, in one quick swoop, grabbed me round the waist and plonked me on his lap. I haven't sat on a man's lap for about three years. Then, I tried to imagine James doing the same thing to me and the improbability of it gave me the giggles, which made Aaron poke me to be quiet, which of course made me giggle even more. It took me a while to compose myself, during which a young girl got up to read some poetry which was actually pretty good. Then I realised I had already been sitting on Aaron's lap for some time and thought it would be rude to get up now. Besides, Aaron was comfortable and I felt very secure as he had one arm around my waist to stop me from falling off. We watched the rest of the show while drinking the second bottle of wine.

Aaron drank much more than me but when I stood up at the end, I realised that I was feeling decidedly light-headed. In fact the whole world was spinning. So I excused myself to go to the bathroom, where I learned that the toilet seat was in fact much further down than I previously thought and as a consequence I think I have a rather attractive bruise on my left buttock. When the world had slowed its spinning down a little, I decided that I, Helen Sloane, had not had this much fun in a long time. So I decided to have another drink. I think it was around this point that I started to hiccup.

Hang on, I need a moment to take some more painkillers . . .

I went back upstairs, where the crowd had thinned out a little and Aaron pulled me over to this little corner table, all shadows with some candles flickering and we start to talk . . . and talk . . . and talk. The café was beautiful and different; someone had written poems all over the walls in large italic script and now some angst-filled woman singer was pouring out her heart through the speakers and the lights were down low. Aaron and I could have talked all night, at least that's how I felt, but I can't remember anything much about what we were talking about. It seemed we discussed everything we could ever think of. Aaron told me all about Nietzsche and some of the books he'd been reading. And he told me about his now not being a Christian; he said that it wasn't that he didn't believe in God any more, which, in a way, he wishes was the case because it would make life much easier for him. He said again that he had never felt like a Christian and that he has no idea what kind of person he would be if he was one. Then he said that he didn't think he'd like himself very much if he became the kind of Christian he grew up thinking he had to be. And the thing is I completely understood him, or at least I did last night. I started to tell him how I sometimes felt like

I was living in two completely different worlds, with completely different rules, and I had to be two totally different people and how I was exhausted by it all and didn't want to morph into Mrs Hemming when I was old and grey.

I think I blurted out that it's all very well proclaiming that you are some sort of spiritual warrior on a Sunday morning during a worship service, but you hardly feel that holy when you're up to your eyes in paperwork and you've got deadlines to meet. The church says pray and things will change, but I said that when I pray about work issues, like Hayley, then nothing ever seems to happen. I started telling him what a little brat Hayley was and about how I was trying to help her but she didn't appreciate it and how I'd felt like I'd prayed all I could for her but nothing had happened. He seemed to be on her side a bit too much, but he spoke about how sometimes it can take years for someone to change, deeply change, and that Christians always seem to expect instant transformation, (especially for themselves), thinking that God will hit them like a strike of lightning and turn them into Mother Teresa overnight. He said that maybe that does happen sometimes, but mostly change is hard work, and that shouldn't scare us because perhaps that means it's more lasting. He told me that if he were to make a decision to become a Christian again he knew it would take a long journey to get there, but that didn't scare him because he knew that the long trek would prove that his decisions were entirely genuine and well thought through.

Then I think we had another glass of wine and we started messing around and doing impressions of some of the people in the CU at university. We talked about how they were always calling meetings to discuss some spiritual crisis or another, which was actually much ado about nothing. Aaron admitted that it was actually at one of those meetings where he began to lose his faith. He said the CU was going to boycott the Spring Ball because the organisers had hired a palm reader who was to be parked in a tent outside the dining-room. They thought this was completely unacceptable and that either the Ball Committee should get rid of the tent or there would be a three line whip that meant that no members of the CU would show up at the Ball. Aaron said that he thought this was fair enough, but he'd suggested that instead of either not going, or getting rid of the tent and making everyone angry at them, that they should set up a prayer tent next to the palm reader and see who had the most effect. It was at that point that he realised that most people in the room didn't seem to believe that prayer would actually have any measurable effect at all – that prayer was something that Christians did because it was right, not because it was effective and potentially life-changing. But, Aaron said, if Jesus had sat in that tent, there would have been a queue stretching halfway around the building. It's obvious that however much Aaron has fallen out of love with Christians, he still is a big fan of Christ – at least at a distance.

'Helen, even though I suggested the prayer tent idea, I would have been scared stiff to sit in it – and why is it that in a CU of hundreds of people, there was not one person who seemed to think that it might be an exciting, dynamic thing to do? We are called to be Christlike but it seems to be so hard that nobody is even coming close. I'm angry at God for making it so easy for us all to fail . . . '

I think he said some more angry stuff but by that point, although I could definitely see his lips moving, I wasn't completely sure what he was saying, which didn't seem to matter because he didn't seem to know what he was saying either. At one point I realised that for the last five minutes I had been fixated on his moving lips and thinking about what it would be like to kiss them and trying to remember what kissing him was like a decade ago. Suddenly he announced that the café was in fact kicking us out. With my mind still somewhat focussed on the idea of kissing, I suggested that we go back to the bookshop and have a nightcap. It had started to rain and by this time I was feeling decidedly light-headed. On the way to the store, which wasn't far, we were twirling our way round lamp-posts reciting some stupid made-up poetry. Or at least I hope Aaron was making it up.

It happened halfway through Aaron yelling out 'I'm so high, in the sky, oh why, oh why, I want to crrrrrrry . . . ' We happened to be whirling around the same lamp post and before I knew it we were suddenly leaning against a brick wall outside the bookshop, engaging in some majorly heavy kissing. We are talking some major passion here, major. He certainly never kissed like this when we were at Uni – because if he had, I would never have forgotten it.

And then Aaron suggested we go inside for some peppermint liqueur he'd picked up whilst picking grapes in France and before I knew it, we were lying on the sofa in the back room and suffice it to say that we were now seriously risking the possibility of becoming surgically glued together.

It's all a bit of a blur now, but I definitely remember this bit, partly because it's completely and utterly humiliating, and partly because either God or Aaron saved me from doing some very unhelpful things. We were mid-way through a conversation and I think I was slurring something about how I was so fed-up with church, not to mention that horrible letter from Mrs Hemming. Like Aaron. I was saying that I completely understood feeling angry about how difficult being a Christian is and that it's awful when you seem to try so hard all the time yet end up messing everything up. And suddenly I felt completely overwhelmed and hopeless in a 'What-the-heck, what's the point in trying?' kind of way and I fell off the sofa in a drunken sprawl. And that's when Aaron got to his feet, adjusted his clothing and said in a slight slur, 'Time to get you home, Helen of Troy.' He helped me retrieve one of my shoes from under the sofa, hauled me out the door and walked me home. I'm not sure who was leaning on whom. Then, after unlocking my front door for me (I seemed to have a slight depth perception problem) he kissed me on the forehead, told me I was very lovely and staggered off down the street.

I must erase all memories of this man from my brain. For starters, he is not a Christian and also he seems to be a terribly bad influence on me. But then again, what kind of good did I do him? This is the man who dumped me the last time I got drunk and then a decade later, I meet up with him, he's retired from faith and I get drunk again and pour out all my troubles about church and morality and Lord knows what else, because I can't completely remember . . .

I must have an incredibly cold shower and clean the flat. And I must stop smelling the jumper I wore last night that still smells of Aaron.

## SUNDAY APRIL 8th

It's been a whole week and I still feel bad about last weekend and Aaron, despite all my Bible reading about forgiveness (a concordance comes in handy). Who knows, I might be the only Christian that he knows these days and what kind of example was I? If anything, he's probably thinking that I'm another good example of faith gone wrong.

Church good. Kristian led worship but then opened his mouth in between songs and shared twaddle. Then I had a lovely lunch with Mum and Dad – but she started on about Bshach Yabba again and that reminded me of how I'd bumped into Aaron. Sad that Aaron hasn't called, but rather glad he hasn't called too because that would potentially make things difficult.

I decided to try to distract myself from my issues by quizzing Dad about the Battle of the Spa – he's still plugging away trying to call a public meeting, but has come up against all kinds of internal resistance. I can't decide if Dad is now someone who believes in dark conspiracy theories, or whether the Council really is as ridden with corruption as he suggests. James talked to me about which computer games we should make available in the youth club. I said that I thought it would be helpful if we could have a selection that didn't require drive-by-shooting, drug deal exchanges, or running people over and gaining points for doing it. 7 days to big conference, which is good, as I am hoping to use the space to gain some sanity.

One other piece of good news – Katy has volunteered to help at the youth club, which made me glad and sad. I've always had her tagged as a slightly air-headed and wafty dancer at the church – and here she is, wanting to help me out. I am judgemental and generally all round bad.

## SUNDAY APRIL 15th

Another whole week gone by and I feel a tiny bit better about life, but not much. All the Bible verses I found about sexual sins and wayward women didn't help – a concordance is a terrible weapon when you use it against yourself. I actually plucked up the courage to talk to Nola about my disastrous Aaronic date. She was kind and understanding and said that, while I'd been foolish and could have placed myself in a vulnerable position, I should be grateful that Aaron was a gentleman. I'm sad that, out of the two of us, he should get the award for the better behaviour.

I have a totally mad week coming up as I have to get ready for taking off for Together for the Kingdom next weekend, which means that (a) I need to make sure that I have bought new and incredibly attractive Arctic thermal gear usually worn by people who hang around with huskies and cook with walrus fat and (b) also need to get slimline small Bible as chugging around from seminar to seminar with my huge Amplified Version might have calorific advantages but is too much effort.

I'm looking forward to it. Some people knock these big Christian events and tag them as unreal, escapist jamborees, but for me and so many others, they're a great opportunity to recharge the batteries, enjoy the excitement of worshipping with thousands – and also graze the gazillion books and CDs available.

There are certain dangers, however, and not just from the cutting breeze that blasts in from the North Sea. One's eyesight can at times be in danger from low flying flags wafted by over enthusiastic flag and banner wavers. Our church is not into flags in worship, except for one lady who sometimes stands at the front with a morose-looking face while swishing a ribbon backwards and forwards with the flair of a windscreen wiper. Hopefully the Lord appreciates her waving at him. Whenever I see her, I think of that verse from the Psalms somewhere that says that the army of the Lord is terrible with banners. She's certainly terrible with a banner . . .

The other slight danger can be overload. If you're not careful, you can dash from workshop to celebration to seminar to debate and end up with a head and heart so stuffed of ideas that you feel like you're mentally constipated. I love words, but Christian events can make me feel like I'm being buried under an avalanche of ideas and, after a while, the words don't mean anything at all. That's why I try to get off the site at least three times a week and go and play with the slot machines in the arcade, or visit a pub, or do anything that's just . . . normal.

Kristian is going and shared last Sunday morning that he's written a couple of new songs in the hope that 'the Lord might give him a platform for wider exposure'. Sometimes when he talks like that, I feel like pushing him off of a platform in front of a passing train.

James is going too and, true to form, is volunteering to help in one of the venues with the sound equipment. He's also the person who collects the booking forms for everybody and books the chalets at the event. This is good, not only for the eternal purposes of the Kingdom of Heaven but also as, hopefully, he will be so engrossed with all his serving that I won't see him too much and that's good because, these days, he seems to look at me with a 'I know what you've been up to' look. Perhaps it's my imagination.

Speaking of James, in his capacity as group organiser, he handed me a sticker for my car today that says 'I'm going to Together for the Kingdom', which I'm supposed to slap on my back bumper. I am having a very minor crisis about the application of this sticky appendage, as it seems a bit odd to announce to other drivers where you're going, as if they care. Not only that, but the sticker has a dove on it too, which announces that the driver is a Christian. And when I'm driving (hideous confession coming) I'm not sure that I always want other drivers to know that I am Christian, especially if I've just cut them up and shared a gesture of greeting. I gave up stickers when I decided to remove the 'In the event of the rapture, this car will be driverless' sticker back in 1995 because (a) I don't think I believe in a rapture and (b) if there was one and suddenly drivers were snatched from their motors, I don't think that other drivers would be terribly interested in sticker reading, but would be more preoccupied with avoiding wildly swerving and out of control cars. I decided to 'forget' to put the sticker on.

Vanessa is going to Together for the Kingdom too. She loves these big events and always goes absolutely ballistic in worship when she's there. This can be somewhat startling for those who come from smaller, quieter churches, especially when Vanessa moves into a time of shrill, high-pitched Latvian yodelling as she calls for the freedom of the people of that land, which she did last year. She also does this rather strange charismatic dance thing where she twirls round and round while hopping up and down and punching the air, which makes her look like she is absolutely desperate to use the loo and has just won the FA cup. Last year when she did the dancing/yodelling thing, one of the stewards was so alarmed, he radioed for assistance from St Johns Ambulance. Vanessa also takes a stack of what she describes as 'worship accessories' along. These include a rain stick, ten packets of incense, some maracas from Brazil and a large map of the world which she has laminated so that she can stand on the various countries while praying, although Israel (for which she likes to pray a lot) is a tough one: being so small, she has to stand on tiptoe. She'd also like to take her large oil drum with her. Sometimes during intercession at her church's prayer meetings, she daubs her face in rainbow-coloured face paint, *Braveheart* style, and beats the living daylights out of this empty oil drum which is painted red for some symbolic reason that I forget. But, thankfully, the oil drum won't fit into the car. I pray that the Lord never provides her with a trailer.

Nola and Robert are going, which is nice, because they'll have the chance to listen and be fed themselves rather than them having to give out.

And hooray, Mr and Mrs Hemming are *not* going, predictably, because, as Mrs Hemming says loudly every year, these interdenominational gatherings are hotbeds of compromise. The Hemmings have been a lot quieter since the difficult meeting with Robert, but I think it's the calm before the storm – something is brewing. Mr Hemming tried to insist that he preach in the church while Robert's away at the conference and (so Nola told me – she probably shouldn't have but there you go) Robert said that, considering the recent difficulties, this would be inappropriate. Mrs Hemming waded in (the first time she's actually spoken to Robert since the showdown) and tried to add her not inconsiderate weight to the argument, but Robert stood his ground and refused. Well done, Robert.

## MONDAY APRIL 16th

Bumped into James in the coffee shop at lunchtime and he asked me if I'd applied my sticker. I told him I hadn't got around to it yet.

Traffic jams tend to make an atheist out of me. I want to be able to speak at great big trucks and command them 'Be thou removed and cast into the depths of the sea' but it doesn't ever work. And although I've been so looking forward to going to this event, the crawling traffic meant that I did a lot of thinking today and that made me feel worse. I'm now almost certain that whoever is speaking at the opening celebration will stop suddenly in the middle of the sermon, point straight at me, speak my full name ever so slowly and loudly and announce to the crowd that a loose woman is in their midst. The drummer will do a melodramatic roll which will then turn into the kind of beat they play before the murderer is executed, a spotlight will slam blinding light straight into my eyes and the stewards will hand out stones to everyone in order to facilitate the public execution. I will die, sobbing and bloody and sorry, but with no opportunity to offer tearful, repentant last words. I will breathe my last, the stewards will remove my limp yet still warm body from the Big Top and then they'll invite the band to come back, do another song and take the offering.

Obviously it's when I'm driving that I daydream the most and that dark little fantasy was giving me a cold sweat, but the fact is that I do feel so guilty again – but I've noticed that my guilt is selective, which is odd. I do feel really bad, not so much about what happened with Aaron and what I wanted to happen, but I have to face it: what I'm sure *would* have happened if Aaron hadn't refused to take advantage of me.

I realised too that, although I thought that Aaron was bad influence on me (and of course in a way he was, because he helped me to chug down half a vineyard's annual harvest of wine), the truth is that on that sofa in the bookshop I was potentially the bad influence on *him*.

So, going back to the selective guilt thing, strangely, I feel terrible about the sex thing, but don't feel that bad about getting out of my head. Why is it that Christians almost sprint their way into huge guilt whenever they feel that they might have compromised even a little bit sexually, but don't have the same capacity for feeling guilty when they lie, gossip, are lazy or lack discipline with what they eat and drink?

Now am feeling guilty because I have a confused capacity for guilt. This is getting worse. I do hope that I have a cataclysmic encounter with God this week that somehow that will sort out all this mess and not involve me being pummelled with stones.

At last I saw the camp's flag, so I parked my car, found a trolley and went looking for my chalet, which is always an agony for two reasons. First, I was loaded up like a pack mule with three plastic carrier bags cutting into my fingers like cheese wire. But the other pain was seeing all these other Christians arriving and unloading. Just looking at them makes me suspect that they don't have the same worries and sins and fears and, unlike me, they don't have to worry about James being in love with me and my odd Mum sometimes and lovely barking mad Vanessa and Aaron with the gin and Kristian with the lovely grin and Hayley the poor, sad, vicious, wounded little cow and Mr and Mrs Hemming . . .

. . . all the other arriving pilgrims at Together for the Kingdom look confident, happy and connected to God with spiritual broadband. They probably sang hymns in the car on the way here today. They know where they're going in life. I can't even find the right block of chalets, because I'm tired and the idiot who created the big map of the site cunningly hid my chalet block out sight.

*Dear God, here I am. Helen. Sloane. It's me and just as I've staggered across the site today with my bags and groceries and extra chocolate biscuits and those plastic shopping bags from hell, so I come to you with all my stuff.*

*Jesus, you say your burden is easy. Mine isn't. Can we do a swap?*

Have to get ready to go to the opening meeting. Hoping no stones being prepared.

### Midnight

I survived the opening celebration without becoming a victim of capital punishment. James is working a late evening venue on the sound desk and Vanessa has gone off to the 24/7 prayer tent with her laminated map, so I decided to have an early night. I am surprised to report that, despite nodding off because of the long drive and the less than riveting sermon from Romans chapter 4 (an odd choice for an opening night), I did like this evening. I decided to tell God that I would worship him, but that I had nothing to say. I'm too tired and a bit too confused to string a sentence together. So I was so relieved when the worship leader decided to lead us all in a beautiful piece of liturgy. As the words came up on the screen, I realised that, when I don't have words, I can take the words that have been written, perhaps hundreds of years ago, by another fellow traveller and I can make their words my own. Feel strangely hopeful about this.

Jesus. Don't know what to say, so I'll just say your name. Over and over. Jesus. Jesus. Jesus.

Goodnight.

## SUNDAY APRIL 22nd

Question: if I decide to tell someone that I think they need to seriously reconsider their attitude towards something, does that make me as bad as Mrs Hemming? Earlier on, Vanessa and I were in one of the cafés on the site and Kristian meandered over and plonked himself down and started going on and on about the young man who led worship for the Bible study in the Big Top this morning, I think his name was Jamie or something. He was very good, he even took us through another piece of liturgy which was very beautiful and he even stopped the music whilst we were doing it so we could concentrate. I never realised it could be so powerful, must ask Robert and Nola if we can do a similar thing in our church. Kristian was going on and on about how great this guy was, though he wasn't too sure about the liturgy idea, wasn't the point of worship to sing? But he mentioned that he was sure that Jamie would want to meet him if he knew that someone with a similar anointing was also here. Vanessa was staring moon-eyed off into the distance, muttering something about somebody's hair being like a flock of goats, whilst Kristian raved on about this guy.

But the strangest thing about it was that on one hand Kristian was saying how great Jamie was, yet on the other hand he was deriding a lot of his music and pretty much insinuating that he thought he could do a much better job. It was obvious:

Kristian couldn't deny Jamie's talent – but he wanted to take his place. Eventually he started saying some nasty things about the guy, which I found distasteful, and I tried to change the conversation three times until he finally spotted someone he knew (I think that probably happens a lot to Kristian at Christian conferences) and he bounced off to embrace them in a big hug.

*Lord, I want to tell Kristian about his envious and unkind attitude. But how do I do it without making him feel as upset as I felt when Mrs Hemming wrote me that letter? Please give me wisdom to know what to do.*

### 11pm

If I knew Kristian was going to turn out to be such a creep, I wouldn't have bothered trying to tell him he shouldn't have been so horrible about that worship leader, Jamie. We were sitting in my chalet and Vanessa and James had gone out to get ice-cream, and I was tentatively trying to bring up the conversation wc had earlier. Which was ironic, as earlier on I couldn't get him to stop talking and now I couldn't get him to start. I thought that if I could get him to say something horrible again by bringing up the subject, I could use that as an example to demonstrate my point. Sneaky I know, but God did tell us to be as cunning as snakes . . .

I managed to get around to the subject again, and he immediately started saying that even though he did like the guy, he thought he was arrogant and that maybe someone else, someone more humble, would be better suited to leading the worship in the Big Top. He said that he got the impression that Jamie was enjoying the whole performance thing too much and celebrity in Christian culture was completely against God's will. By which point I got angry, I didn't think the guy was like that at all. If anything he seemed shy. So I started saying that I didn't think he should be so critical of him and that I'm sure he didn't ask to be treated like a celebrity, the way that some Christians treated him – and I was looking pointedly at Kristian as I said it, as I know he got Jamie to sign three CDs and his Bible yesterday . . .

Then suddenly, without word or warning, Kristian lunged towards my face and in a second started slobbering all over my mouth, pushed me back down on the couch and tried a sneaky move with his hands.

I was in shock. I tried to move away but he was pushing me down so in the end there was nothing else for it: I had to knee him in the stomach. What is wrong with me? Do I ooze some sort of sexual signal to men that screams I'm easy? He's a worship leader, for goodness sake, but I got the distinct impression that he had done this kind of thing before. I bet that Jamie guy would never do anything like that. Anyway I pushed him off and in a firm, okay, admittedly shaky voice, I told him politely that it was definitely time to leave. And that if he ever tried anything like that again, I wouldn't hesitate about telling Robert and Nola. Of course he looked absolutely petrified. I wonder if a girl has ever refused him before . . . he started apologising, saying that he thought that was what I wanted . . .

. . . and then he went into verbal attack mode. He said that by being alone in a chalet with him late at night, I had led him on and caused him to stumble. Can you believe that idiot? I was about to resort to the use of my emergency swear word when, thankfully, James and Vanessa appeared outside with ice-cream. Kristian is a phoney. I was mad ever to like him.

The blond blue-eyed *Abba* children will never, ever materialise. At least one issue in my life is sorted once and for all. Kristian Vivian Rogers is history.

## MONDAY APRIL 23rd

I went to a seminar about doubt today. The speaker did absolutely nothing for me whatsoever and frankly I didn't understand most of what he was saying but, to be honest, that might have more to do with me than his presentation. I can hardly think straight because I'm still so angry about last night. 'I want to be a big Christian star' Kristian hasn't been seen by anyone today – it's like he's hiding away, probably worried sick about what I might say, especially if I decide to tell Robert and Nola. My mind's in a whirl because I've got this idea that I'm emanating some signal to men – after all, I was ready to get into some serious pash with Aaron, ended up completely off my head, and then within a few days find myself in a clinch with the worship leader 'goddette'. I think I hate him for his pretentious arrogant attitude and then his totally unsubtle come-on – but I think I hate myself more and wonder if I'm fooling myself and that I'm sending out signals to the entire male population of planet Earth, inviting them to come hither and ravish me.

I was turning all of these ideas around endlessly in my head – my brain feels like a washing machine full of smelly socks – when my attraction was distracted by one particular steward. I've been watching these stewards over the last couple of days and 99% of them are nothing short of wonderful. They work long hours and the majority of them keep smiling and are patient and kind. Admittedly there is one large bearded bloke with a walkie-talkie who is obviously delighted to be in power and he's so gruff and rude, I think he'd be chucked out of the Gestapo for being too rough. He barked at me yesterday for leaving my Bible in the aisle. It was a health and safety hazard, he said, didn't I know that someone could trip up over that Bible and seriously hurt themselves? Of course, he's right – it was a little careless of me – but he didn't need to bark at me like an Alsatian on speed and make me feel like the Witch of Endor just because I was a bit absent-minded with my pocket-sized NIV. I apologised, but he muttered something and then started yelling into his walkie-talkie with a voice one would expect a Secret Service agent to use if the President had been shot. The reason for his screaming was that the venue was running out of chairs. I noticed that when extra chairs were brought in, he did nothing to help the other stewards to put them out. He's loud, rude and lazy with it. I'm trying to resist the temptation to use my 'smite him with boils' prayer on him.

All of which makes the steward I was watching today even more wonderful. He is incredible. A couple of people came in late and wanted seats at the front, which were all taken. He had to tell them there was no room and they started yelling about paying good money to come to this conference and you can't even get a seat. He flushed red with embarrassment but still held his cool and then went out of his way to find them two seats together nearer the back. They didn't even thank him. They were the last two seats available too.

But then a man with a very large Bible and a huge notebook appeared – he looked like a very serious, scholarly type and when that same steward had to kindly tell him that the venue was full and fire regulations meant that no-one else could be accommodated, the serious deep notebook clutcher went off on one and started on about how he was going to complain because this seminar was on his specialist area of interest and it was so unfair that he couldn't get in and someone should plan these things more effectively and he was going to take this up with someone in authority. The steward apologised. It was then that the deep scholar sneered at him and said, 'Your apology doesn't count. You're just a steward. I need to take this issue up with someone in authority.'

And then the steward apologised yet again, whereupon the man stomped out of the tent. I was tempted to follow the rude angry idiot out of the tent and fell him to the ground with one expertly delivered judo kick (which probably wouldn't happen as my only initiation into the dark skills of martial arts was watching the *Karate Kid* when I was ten) but instead I realised that I needed to find the steward at the end of the seminar and apologise to him. I felt that these pompous idiots' rudeness reflected on all the delegates at the conference. Then I wondered if I was just expanding my seemingly never-ending capacity for guilt again, but at last when the speaker had sat down and the seminar closed, I wandered over to the steward, who impossibly was still smiling and saying goodbye to delegates as they left the tent.

'I wanted to say how sorry I am about that man's rudeness to you and thank you for all your hard work', I stammered out, wondering if he would think that I was mad.

But the opposite happened. His smile got even bigger and we chatted for a while. I found out that sometimes he even comes to this conference as a speaker. His name is Jim and he's a consultant professor of business studies. He has a top job, but loves to come and offer his time freely as a steward when he's not speaking. He's probably got a brain three times the size of the deep notebook clutcher. Most of his time is spent in the children's venues, he said. As a dad and grandfather, he loves to see the children learning about God.

What a contrast to the 'I want to be an international worship superstar' attitude of horrid Kristian.

I came away from the seminar, a little exhausted from all my internal wrangling and still slightly worried that I am in fact related to the whore of Babylon, but inspired and encouraged by watching Jim and chatting with him for a while. Some people can't help being a blessing.

## TUESDAY APRIL 24th

**8am**

Got up super extra early to pray, go running and generally be holy. That incident with Kristian has made me feel terrible. I feel like I've done something wrong, even though I'm sure I haven't. I keep running the incident through in my mind. Maybe I've misjudged the situation and it wasn't as bad as it seemed. I feel that if I was a better person, this wouldn't have happened to me.

*Lord, please take this feeling away. Perhaps kissing Aaron put some sort of horrible thing in my life and Kristian was picking up on that. Lord, I know I've already asked you this, but please forgive me.*

**6pm**

I am writing this in a café, trying not to let my tears drip on the keyboard, but I'm okay. I've had an emotional afternoon and in some ways the outcome is depressing, but I have also managed to resolve a few important issues. I now feel like an independent woman who has a firm grip on her life. Okay, it's more like a loose finger grip on a greased pole, but nonetheless it is a grip. James turned up at my chalet this afternoon and after shuffling around at the door for a bit, finally asked if I would like to go for coffee. Of course, when he said coffee, he might as well have said marriage, children and matching coffins. Why is asking someone for coffee in Christian circles such a big deal? I wondered whether, if I decided to go, I was somehow committing myself to a lifelong relationship of sound desk support and folding James's underpants?

Anyway, I decided that this thought was far too neurotic and told James that although I didn't fancy a coffee, I wouldn't mind trying one of those vanilla and chocolate milkshakes I saw them selling yesterday. On the way there, we bumped into Vanessa who gave us a fleeting smile and hurried off to what was probably her eleventh seminar, workshop or preach that day. We sat down. James bought the milkshake. I panicked. Does letting James buy me a milkshake mean that we are now in a committed relationship leading to marriage? I decided for a moment that James was lovely and wondered what it would be like to kiss him, but then my mind rebelled and I found myself imagining kissing Aaron instead. Hormones sometimes have no discipline. Anyway, while I was imagining kissing Aaron, (well, not imagining, more replaying) I suddenly realised that James was looking at me like he expected an answer to an important question. I am a terrible person, sitting across the table with what could be my future husband imagining kissing some agnostic bookshop worker who has, I suspect, a burgeoning drink problem.

'Sorry, I wandered off there, what was the last bit? I asked him. He looked instantly dismayed.

'The thing is Helen, you see, I don't want to put, um, any sort of pressure on you and if you would prefer not to answer today, then, um, I guess that's fine. Because I know you might be confused at the moment because of some people' (with this he clenched his jaw) 'but you see I was wondering whether you could tell me whether you thought anything would ever, um, happen between us. No pressure or anything, it might be good for me to know, because I've kind of noticed some tension between us. And of course I could be completely wrong, but I thought I would tell you that I kind of like you and wondered whether you, um, liked me too?'

I looked into his face and it was the face of lovely James who, yes, would make a great husband and a fantastic father. James, a good man and a man who loves God. And suddenly I had this realisation, something dawned and I looked at James in an entirely new light.

You see I have had a revelation. The reason I had never resolved my feeling for James is because I never believed that God had anyone else out there for me. I thought that James was my one chance and that the reason why I didn't fancy him was because there was something wrong with me. There is no spiritual reason why I don't fancy James; I don't fancy James because well, I don't fancy James. It doesn't mean there's anything wrong with him, or that there's anything wrong with me either. It is how it is.

This took me some time to realise and by then James looked like he was either going to burst into tears or was passing something particularly tricky through his lower intestine. So at last I spoke.

'James, I think you're a lovely man. I think you're kind and loyal and godly. But I don't think that we were meant for each other. I'm sorry. I think there are another couple of people out there somewhere who would be incredibly disappointed if we decided to get together.'

James looked a little bit too relieved for my liking.

'Oh, ok. I guess that's that then. This hasn't got anything to do with Kristian, has it? Because, Helen, I'm saying this because I'm your friend. I don't think I trust him.'

'I know', I replied. 'Don't worry, I am never going to go near Kristian Rogers again.'

James looked relieved. And suddenly jumped up.

'Listen Helen, I'd better go, because there's a seminar I said I'd go to with Vanessa. No hard feelings, yeah? I hope we can still be friends without feeling awkward around one another.'

'Sure' I smiled and kissed him on the cheek. 'No problem.'

He left. I thought that if that man doesn't believe things are going to awkward, then he has the emotional intelligence of a wombat. Things were going to be as awkward as King Herod being the Director of the Bethlehem Playgroup Society. And then the strangest thing happened. I started to cry. Though I felt better for having resolved this situation with James, from his side anyway, I felt a little lost. I have one horrible man who likes me a little too much for comfort, (or at least tried to like me a little too much for comfort), I have one lovely man who, try as hard as I can, I can't seem to like back and I have one super sexy guy and I don't want to date him because he isn't a Christian. I am officially a failure with men. I looked around the coffee shop and all I seemed to see were wedding rings, I mean people fall in love all the time. How hard can it be?

Then suddenly a smiling woman came up to my table, wearing a steward's coat and a big badge on her lapel that says *Counsellor*. Uh oh, I immediately thought, because I've always thought it was a bit strange that Christians seem so eager to tell their deepest, darkest secrets to people they don't even know. She asked me if I was alright and I tried to hold back the tears and say that I was fine. But it came out in a bit of a wail and I ended up telling her about everything – about Kristian and James and Aaron. About how I didn't know if I believed that God had a husband for me and that no man would ever love me anyway because I am clearly a Jezebel and am not the kind of girl who would ever be allowed to sing in the backing group for a worship leader . . .

'It seems to me' she said, after I had finally stopped hiccupping in her lap, 'that just because you've done something you regret, doesn't mean that you're broadcasting that fact to every man in the universe. And secondly, if you're not that great, then why does an amazing man like James seem to like you so much? Helen, maybe your problem is that you spend far too much time arguing with God.' Then she prayed for me and offered to spend more time with me but I said it was ok. To be honest, I was annoyed at this point, because I don't think that I argue with God. I'm always asking him to tell me what to do and trying to obey him. I may get things wrong sometimes, but I never argue! This is why it's such a bad idea to pour your heart out to some stranger, who probably got married when they were 19 anyway and who has no idea what it's like to be 27 and single. But, strangely, I still do feel a little better about everything now. *Lord, please keep working in my life. Sort out my head. And my heart. Amen.*

## At bedtime

Slighty iffy news: still no sign of Kristian. I am slightly worried, but I think he's lying low to give it a day or so for things to blow over. Bad news (I think): James seems perfectly okay with my telling him that nothing's going to happen between us. It's funny really, because that's exactly what I want, it's even what I've prayed for – but it would be helpful if he'd appear ever so slightly disappointed . . .

Good news: I think that I've actually made a serious step forward tonight in my *I'm a wicked witch and I'm broadcasting lust vibes to every man on Earth* hang-up. Despite all the criticisms of these mega-Christian events, I actually think that I've met God today and that a lot of things are falling into place.

I became increasingly angry after that counsellor woman told me I argued with God. What a nerve. I went back to my chalet and read the story of Jacob wrestling with God. It took a long time, because of my using the Amplified Version that I borrowed from Vanessa (Jacob wrestled, fought, struggled with, contested with God, the Lord, Yahweh, Jehovah). Okay, I get the point. But I don't get the point of that comment. I do make loads of mistakes, but this wrestling idea seems to mean that I am fighting what God wants to do in my life. Half my angst is the fact that I do want God's will for me. In fact, sometimes I envy Laura's uncomplicated way of living. She doesn't worry about eternity, God's will, the world, angels, demons and a host of other things that fill my head – she gets on with living. Anyway, I spent some time telling God that I don't think that I argue with him, but I am willing to be shown that I argue with him if I do, because I don't want to argue with him about arguing with him . . .

Felt more confused than ever and so I was not looking forward to the service tonight. I chuntered my way all the way through the worship, took exception to the song choice, wrote the woman off who was going to preach as a token Christian woman leader (and then realised that with an attitude like that, no-one can win – when there's not a woman up there, we get mad and when there is, we write her off as token). I realised that sometimes people get upset with things that happen in churches and conferences but the issues that they complain about are not the real issues at all. They're not happy and are finding ways to express their unhappiness – anything will do.

I'd pretty much written off the evening as worthless, when the lady who was preaching started into her talk. She took me off my guard, because she was warm, funny and very vulnerable. She opened up the sermon by telling us about some ridiculous things that she'd done – and some mistakes that she'd made. I immediately liked her, because here was someone who is obviously passionate about God and heading in the right direction, but isn't afraid to admit that she trips up too. And then she got down to the business of opening up the Scripture text, which was that bit about Peter having a dream where God lowers a sheet full of non-kosher animals and commands highly Jewish Peter to snack from it. The preacher lady said that as Peter was a good kosher boy, this was the cultural equivalent of God lowering a full stocked bar into a Salvation Army service on a Sunday morning and saying 'The drinks are on me, ladies and gentlemen' – and so understandably Peter refused. And then God said to Peter, 'Don't call unclean what I've called clean' – and so Peter did as he was told.

The preacher lady told the story hilariously and I roared at the way she described the scene – and then suddenly, even as I was laughing, something hit me like a ton of bricks. Peter was arguing with God as he insisted on tagging something as unclean – and that's exactly and precisely what I've been doing with *myself*. God says that I'm clean – and yet I struggle with the idea, think I'm doing God a favour when I beat myself up and even treat forgiveness like a dieter would treat Belgian chocolate – a rather indulgent luxury that I don't deserve, would like but should probably refrain from. I'm like some ancient monk whipping myself and drawing blood and thinking that he's pleasing God as he rips off a bit more flesh – or even a bit like old Simeon up the pole who thought that God was pleased with him for parking in his own filth for years. If God's final and unalterable verdict about me is that I'm clean through what Jesus has done, then who am I to disagree? Arguing with God is not just about wicked rebellion and refusal to do his will – it's also about refusing to accept his blessings and gifts of love.

Anyway, at the end of the sermon the preacher lady brought out a huge, beautifully packaged gift tied with rich gold ribbon – and talked about how sad a father would be if he'd sacrificed hugely to make sure that his son or daughter could enjoy a gift – but they refused to even open or accept it. We needed to repent of our guilty arguing, she said. I cried buckets – for the second time today – and went forward at the end because it was obvious that God was talking to me. I felt bad about my judging the counsellor lady too – obviously she planted a seed in my mind and somehow God pulled it all together. When I went forward, James came out too and stood with me while I prayed, which I thought was nice. Perhaps, even though it is going to be awkward, we can still be friends after all. I hope so.

I got together with Vanessa in the chalet afterwards and told her everything: James, Aaron, the whole sorry mess, but I also explained what had happened today with the counsellor and then the sermon tonight. She was lovely. And unexpectedly clear in her response. She read me the story from the Bible about Peter refusing to allow Jesus to wash his feet – another argument with Jesus, she said and about how Jesus had absolutely insisted that Peter let him do that. She said that Jesus warned Peter that, unless he allowed the foot-washing thing, he could have no part with Jesus. Vanessa said that the only way we can be with Jesus is on the basis of this marvellous arrangement – we allow him to clean us up. Unless we do, this Christian thing won't work. I cried again and it was all rather wonderful, until I suddenly noticed that Vanessa was kneeling down in front of me and tugging at my feet. She'd grabbed a washing-up bowl from the sink and filled it with warm water, added some salt for some symbolic purpose and was now proposing to wash my feet as a reminder of this day. I didn't want to happen, not least because I was wearing tights which means that (a) I'd have to take them off which would be a bit weird or (b) end up with soggy tights which would be worse. Vanessa's trip back to planet Normal was but a brief excursion.

She eventually seemed okay about my not wanting to do the foot-washing thing – at first she rather sternly told me that I was being like Peter in my not wanting a washing, but I then reminded her that Peter was very probably not wearing tights and so he had no excuse. The great thing is that I think I'm starting to realise that forgiveness is not about feelings, about taking advantage of God, or about being a wimpy Christian – grace and forgiveness sit at the heart of everything. When you know that you've been forgiven, then you'll go all the way with God, like Peter did. Maybe he remembered the foot-washing incident after he denied Jesus and the memory of it helped him to finally find peace about his betrayal . . .

I am exhausted from all this emotion and thinking. Good night.

## WEDNESDAY APRIL 25th

### 10am

The mystery of Kristian is no mystery at all. It turns out he's been hanging out with some other girl. They walked past me today and she shot me a look as if I was the biggest weirdo since the Elephant Man. I dread to think what he told her about me – probably that I was completely obsessed about him or something. I've been trying to decide whether or not to talk to Robert and Nola about what happened with Kristian. I know it's not a massively big deal, but I get the feeling that he might try the same thing with another girl in my church, who might not have the presence of mind to do anything about it. I think I'll go find Nola and see what she thinks about the whole situation.

### 1pm

Have just talked to Nola and have also consumed a lunch that would feed a family of five comfortably. She says that she and Robert had already been keeping a close eye on Kristian and that they would pray about what to do about the situation. She said that Robert had already had a quiet word with him about dating girls in the church and that as Kristian is a member of the pastoral team, he must talk it over with Robert before he decides to get 'romantically involved' with anyone. I feel much better now someone has taken this situation out of my hands.

*Thank you, Lord, for Nola and Robert, please give them the wisdom and strength to make the right decisions.*

**4pm**

I began the afternoon by going to a seminar on grief which was awful. I'm not sure why I went really, but it said in the programme that grief is one experience that every human being on planet Earth will have to steer through, so I thought perhaps it would be good to be prepared.

The man who led the seminar said that he understood grief because his cat had died recently, which was sad, but I felt terrible for the people sitting in the audience who were mourning the loss of their children or spouses; comparing their sadness to his seemed ridiculous. Then he started talking about how he'd found comfort in the belief that his cat was now in heaven, which sounded nice and reasonable and then I tried to imagine a ginger tabby in the sky with its paws raised singing *Blessed be the name of the Lord* along with the heavenly choir and then I wondered if rats and lice got to go there too and then I gave up, pretended that I had an urgent text message, left the seminar and met Vanessa for coffee.

Now I have just returned from a songwriters' workshop. Yes. Me, whose untamed voice sounds like a harpy with hiccups, attended a workshop about writing songs. I only went because Vanessa has decided that she would like to write worship songs as well. Apparently everybody wants to get in on the action. However, her efforts so far haven't been too bad, better than Kristian's anyway, which of course isn't hard. She managed to write the lyrics for a whole song yesterday without mentioning mountains, any type of body of water, or repeating the same phrase over and over again.

I am continuously struck by what an amazing woman Vanessa is. She is a bit mad, but part of that seems to be the secret of her success as a human being. She doesn't seem to have the sort of problems I have, although sometimes I know she feels a bit overwhelmed. She talks a lot about the difference between the world as it is now and the Kingdom of God that Jesus spoke about all the time – and it upsets her. She says the amount of suffering in the world is absolutely sickening, especially since we seem to do so little about it. Sometimes she loses the hope that anything can be done at all and thinks that maybe the world should burn up in some kind of apocalyptic inferno. But, when she feels like hopeless, she says she prays a lot more and that after a couple of days things feel better.

This songwriters' workshop put my mind at ease about Kristian. I'd been worrying about the part he plays in church life. I was nervous about what would happen if he did 'make it' and people everywhere started buying and singing his songs. What would I have to do? Stand up at a huge worship conference and announce that he in fact didn't deserve to be there because of his false motives, judgmental attitude – and tendency to lunge at members of his congregation? But who am I to decide who or who does not 'make it'? And by that time he might have made some peace with God, or have completely changed and I would be destroying his career. All this has been niggling me. But now my mind has been put at ease.

The worship workshop was run by worship pundit Graham and Vanessa practically wet herself on the way. She went on and on about this song he wrote called *How long?* which completely changed her life as a Christian. I've personally never heard of it, but I'm sure Vanessa will play it to me, probably over and over again at some point, until I'm forced to ask the question 'How long?' myself.

The workshop was split into two parts. In the beginning Graham talked about worship music, what made a good song and about the kind of songs we should write as songwriters in order to serve the church. It was a good talk and strangely he said everything I'd been thinking for so long in church about worship music! He stressed how we need to be more careful about what lyrics we put in our songs and that we need to be more like poets. He cited a few examples from some old hymns and I suddenly realised how much theological and biblical knowledge those writers managed to cram into one line. He also mentioned that it would be fantastic to hear more songs that spoke about stories in the Bible, at which point Vanessa started bouncing up and down in her seat.

In the second half Graham invited people to share some of the songs they'd written and we all discussed how we thought they could be better, in a very nice Christian way . . .

Just before Kristian got up to share his song, (which I noticed he seemed to have scribbled down during the talk) I noticed Graham leaning over and whispering something in his ear. Suddenly Kristian's face went bright red. Apparently (I heard afterwards from James, there in his role of sound man, sitting next to Kristian) Kris had written a song about the biblical character of Ruth, but in his hurry he'd confused her name with Rahab, Boaz's morally negotiable grandmother. Graham stepped in at the last minute and saved Kris from totally embarrassing himself in front of everyone. Kristian didn't even look that grateful.

Then he sang his song, *I am Ruth*, during which he repeated the line, 'Take me, take me, I breathe you Lord', about twelve times, possibly more, but by that time I had blanked out and was instead trying not to think about kissing Aaron.

When Kris finally ended and looked around the workshop for an expected barrage of applause, there was embarrassed silence, which I think Kristian took as stunned awe, as he moved into his faraway eyes-half-closed and nodding routine and stood there at the mike going, 'Yeah, Lord. Yeah, Jesus. Yeah. Mmm . . . '

It was at this point I realised that the Bride of Christ was safe from Kristian's minor chord fumblings, at least for now. It didn't seem like he was going to go anywhere in worship music very fast which, all in all, I thought was a very good thing. Finally, he sat down.

Vanessa was completely ecstatic because Graham said the song she wrote about King David was excellent and that though it might be better suited as more of a performance song, as he thought a congregation might find it hard to sing, he was sure that people would get a lot out of it.

So, it was an all-round good day for everyone, even Kristian (but in a way that he probably doesn't appreciate). *Thank you, Lord.*

Oh, phoned home to Mum and Dad tonight. My dad seems to be a bit down about this whole business with the Council selling Lawrence House. But despite all that he still managed to encourage me, mainly by the way he listened to all my ramblings. He'd make a great counsellor at one of these events. Whenever I'm upset he always says to me that our troubles can make us strong – if we go to God with them. I think he's right, but I would prefer strength and would like to pass on the troubles.

The rest of the conference was uneventfully nice. I did have a bit of a minor crisis when I went to a session about calling and it seemed to be all about being church leaders or missionaries in some far-flung part of the globe, translating the Bible while existing on a diet of sheep entrails. Had a quirk of guilt again about leaving house group leadership and focussing on the youth club (which opens tomorrow night – *help!*) but remembered Nola's advice about the Kingdom of God.

Drove home and experienced that rather strange deflated feeling that tends to land on me when I get to the end of a nice holiday or a Christian conference. Somehow everything seems slightly greyer when you get home and of course all the atmosphere of the big event is gone too. I've got a feeling that I've spent almost a week in an unreal place and that there's no connection between what I've been in and what I'm in now. But the more I thought about the counsellor/arguing with God/Peter and hoofed animals/Vanessa and her good advice/attempt to hold a ritual hosiery drenching, I decided that what I'd experienced was very real. Read and reread my journal and realised how good it was to have written it all down.

During the drive home, when the local young farmers seemed to have come out onto the roads for a tractor convention, I daydreamed unhelpfully about Aaron. All my holy dealings don't eradicate the moment of that rather terrific snogging session, but I decided that I am not going to contact Aaron for now. I wasn't good for him and he wasn't good for me either – helping me to pickle my liver that night – and anyway, I've decided that if I am going to go somewhere in a relationship, I want it to be with someone who's full-on as a Christian. I've made that decision, not because of something in the Bible about being unequally yoked. To be honest, I'm not totally sure what that's about anyway. It's that I do want someone who can understand this driving urgency that I've got to live for God. I love Laura, but actually I don't want her uncomplicated life: I don't want to live for nothing but the next day. I'm not judging her, but I know that I want more than that. Back to work tomorrow. Looking forward to seeing Laura. Not looking forward to seeing Hayley. 24 hours to the youth club opening!

## FRIDAY APRIL 27th

Back to earth with a huge bump. I did my early morning run and then as soon as I got in to the office, Laura took me to one side and said that there'd been a bad development in Hayley's case – it turns out that Hayley got into some serious self-harming while I was gone and ended up in Casualty. It definitely wasn't a suicide attempt, but she managed to cut herself badly enough to need medical attention. This is new territory for Hayley – she's been an abuser of other people so effectively that she could probably get an honorary doctorate in swearing, but this is the first time, to my knowledge, she's actually turned on herself. To make things worse, apparently she called the office to speak to me while I away last Tuesday, but when the duty social worker said I'd be back in today, she gave them another epic mouthful and slammed the phone down. On Wednesday, her uncle left a message on the office answering machine to say that Hayley had been an outpatient that night, that she'd been fixed up and was back home now and that none of this would have happened if we duffelcoated stuck-ups in Social Services were around to do our jobs. Apparently Hayley had gone back to the bloke in the caravan park and had found him with someone else, which threw her into a mad session with a sharp knife. She's going to be okay, but the scars will be nasty.

Went straight round to her house – but she was out with her friends and so I got yet another tongue-lashing from her dysfunctional guardians. Last week's conference seems like ancient history now. I'm going to reread my journal again now to remind myself of what happened.

### Bedtime

Well, it was a small start, but we've begun. The Council wouldn't let us take down all the old photographs of long dead Councillors that line the walls, so there's a feeling that there are old people glaring at us all the time – but it's okay. We got a small football table, which we bought from the little offering that the house group took on my leaving night. It feels like a classroom, which of course isn't likely to create a line of kids at the door. But we have to start somewhere.

Only seven kids showed up at first, including one of the laddettes who hangs around a lot with Hayley and who said that Hayley had a message for me. She wanted me know that she wouldn't be seen dead in my pathetic little club. That girl is one hurt piranha. I started to get a little bit upset but then got a grip and decided that nothing was going to ruin the first night.

A little bit of stress crept into the evening when another three kids showed up and said that they weren't going to wait their turn for the bleeping pool table because they bleeping well wanted to bleeping play now and if they bleeping well couldn't, well then they'd tell all their bleeping friends what a complete bleeping waste of space this bleeping bleeping bleeping bleeping youth bleeping club was.

I was still smarting from Hayley's nastiness, so I was ready to kick them out on the spot, but James's computers saved the day. He invited them to save planet Earth from an intergalactic monster that was running riot through the subterranean caverns of an underground kingdom by nuking it with a laser. This they did happily and even ended up watching another couple of kids play pool and then took their turn with a compliance which was surely a miracle almost as epic as the raising of Lazarus, although not nearly so smelly.

At the end of the evening, James helped tidy up and then lugged all his computer equipment into the car – he worked hard. When at last we'd locked up, we stood in the car park for a few minutes talking about how the first night had gone and – I might be completely mad here – I'm sure that James was thinking about kissing me, all this despite our little 'clarification' chat at Together for the Kingdom. He stood a little closer than usual and his eyes seemed to be roaming my face as if searching for a hint that it would be okay. And here's the problem – it would have been okay and in fact I wanted to kiss him to thank him for praying for me and for doing the offering at the house group which meant that we had a football table and then coming and helping out at the club. I want to kiss him for all of that, but I don't want to kiss him – for the kiss. I still keep trying to imagine fancying him, but it's like trying to get a decent fire going with damp wood. Anyway, what's the point since we've had our little heart to heart? In the end, I gave him a nice warm and appropriately brief hug of thanks, with three swift pats on the back, and drove home. Perhaps the notion that he wanted to kiss me was my hyperactive imagination.

In church this morning we had one of those 'Let's share what God did for us while we were away at the conference' times, which I'm never sure is a good idea, because it can send a message to those who didn't go that God was so at Together for the Kingdom that they missed it, but that we who went now glow in the dark and are streets ahead in faith from the rest of you. Kristian shared about how he met the Lord at the conference, which almost prompted me to choke, because he so almost met my fist that night in the chalet. He also said that God had given him a song at the conference and that it had made a tremendous impact on everyone, which is so untrue, unless you count those healed of insomnia while he was singing it. Robert spoke on praying for those who need the Lord and I suddenly realised that I had spent more time snogging Aaron than praying for him.

Lunch at Mum and Dad's was a bit traumatic. Lovely to see them again, but Dad was quiet during the meal. Afterwards Mum got on the phone to book a slot with her yoga teacher and so Dad and I went for a walk.

Dad said there is a big meeting at the Town Hall on Saturday about Lawrence House. He said that it is an opportunity for the community to unite against such blatant corruption and claim back something that belonged to them in the first place. He said that the sneaky Council had tried to keep quiet the fact that they were having the meeting, so not many people would come. But he and Mum were trying to pack out the hall. He said there is a chance that if enough people know what they were planning to do, we could shame them into changing their minds. I, of course, said that I will go along and that I will try to get as many of my friends to come as possible.

When I got back to the flat tonight I phoned Vanessa who phoned James who phoned Robert and Nola who phoned most of the church. Nola phoned me just now and said that this is exactly the kind of thing that the local church should be involved in and it is important that the community keep this building. In a fit of madness, I even invited Laura from work, who surprisingly said she'd come. Dave has finally left her. I think she must be feeling a bit lonely.

Also texted Vanessa to say that I want us to get together for lunch tomorrow to talk about praying for people we like or love who don't know God. Like Aaron. And Laura.

## WEDNESDAY MAY 2nd

Vanessa and I have called the prayer meeting. James is coming too. I am actually getting into prayer at the moment. All this running means I have been praying loads, partly for something to do, partly so God can send an army of angels to carry me up the next hill and perhaps provide a water fountain, but mainly to talk to God. The funny thing about praying is that once you start, sometimes it can be difficult to stop. I have been praying so much more recently that sometimes I don't even seem to notice I'm doing it. Sometimes, I'm not even talking out loud or in my head, I'm kind of generally including God in what I'm doing. I find myself saying, look at that tree, isn't it beautiful, or that woman looks sad, please comfort her. Anyway, I've been praying for Laura and Aaron a lot recently and after Robert's talk on Sunday, I felt the need to get together with some other Christians to pray for them some more. *Lord, please give us the right words to say, please let Aaron and Laura see what I see in you.*

I've been reading Psalm 4, which says that some people love delusions. Thinking about Aaron's bookshop today, wondered if that verse applies to some of the stuff in there. Do people love complex, almost illogical ideas because they're not really looking for answers – they get a kick out of asking questions? Then I thought that there's also a very powerful place for questions, one that the church needs to reclaim. Questions can be holy, even when they don't lead us to answers.

Well! What I thought would be a relatively straightforward prayer meeting in Vanessa's living-room ended up with me lurking in an alley outside Aaron's bookshop and hiding behind a bush in Laura's front garden. It all started off pretty normal. Vanessa had baked cheese straws in the shape of little crosses and James had brought along a bottle of grape juice because apparently he knows how much I like the taste of the vineyard. We had been praying for about 40 minutes and I must admit I was getting into it.

So we were praying when suddenly Vanessa had this idea that we should go and pray over the places where Aaron and Laura spend a lot of time. She said that it's important to not only pray over a person but also the place they inhabit, so we should go to both of their houses and reclaim the ground for God. Normally I would be against such ludicrous ideas but for some reason I agreed to go along with this one. James started packing the cheese straws into his pockets for provisions and even produced a flask from somewhere to keep the grape juice in. That man thinks of everything – so we were prepared as we proceeded to go forth and conquer the powers of wickedness, as Vanessa put it.

First, we went to Laura's house, as I have no idea where Aaron lives. We could see her inside through a crack in the curtains. Vanessa wanted to march round the house seven times like Joshua did in the Bible, but James and I managed to dissuade her by saying the walls might fall down and we were trying to bless Laura, not destroy her home. Luckily, Vanessa had come as prepared as Buffy the Vampire Slayer in a graveyard. She had holy oil from Israel, a flask of communion wine, several ornate crosses and a stick of incense.

She instructed me and James to go and hide in a bush and start praying and I'm sure I saw a glimmer of a smirk on her face when she said it. She said she'd go and consecrate the ground by burying a cross that faced the east and pouring communion wine and oil on the heathen flower beds. By that point I had given up protesting, as Vanessa was clearly a woman with a mission – a mission with a capital M, for mad, so I let her get on with it, whilst I half-heartedly prayed for Laura's revelation that Christ was in fact the one true King of the Universe. At the beginning of praying, James said we should hold hands, as it would unite our spirits against the darkness and make us more powerful warriors of Christ. I decided that he and Vanessa had definitely more in common than I had previously thought.

Vanessa took ages and by the time she had come back, my hand was definitely feeling sweaty and we had both run out of things to pray, so we were generally standing in the bushes, holding hands and feeling a bit awkward. At least I was feeling awkward, I kept on wanting to let go of his hand, but then I thought it might offend him so I didn't. I then wandered if he was thinking the same thing and worried that in fact he didn't want to hold my hand either, despite being the one to suggest it, and had started to panic. Luckily Vanessa came back just in time, as I was trying to decide whether to kiss James to see what would happen, or let go of his hand and run away.

Because we didn't know where Aaron lived, we decided to go to the bookshop where he worked and rebuke all the evil spirits that lived there because of the blasphemous reading material inside, according to Vanessa anyway. She kept going on about calling some angel called Tal to build a fortress inside the shop and protect Aaron from the demon of depression. So we made our way to Penny Alley. James and I stood outside the shop for a bit and I think we both felt a bit stupid. By now, even James, who I've never heard say a bad word about anyone (except perhaps Kristian) was looking a bit fed-up. Then I noticed a little alley by the side of the shop and decided to investigate.

I made my way carefully down the shadowy lane, almost breaking my neck on a few boxes, when I noticed that light was spilling out of a little window. I took a quick look and realised Aaron was asleep on the old battered sofa in the back of the shop. I remember that sofa well. His chestnut curls were all mussed up on the arm of the sofa and he had an almost empty bottle of gin falling out of his left hand onto the floor.

His shirt was off and I suddenly had a huge rush of feeling for him. I wanted to hug him and never let go. I thought maybe I could help him get over whatever it was he was going through. I also noticed there was a smouldering cigarette in the ashtray and started desperately praying that the bookshop wouldn't burn down. I so wanted him to be safe. As I stumbled back up the alley, I bumped straight into James. Vanessa was standing there too, having anointed all four corners of the shop doorway with oil.

'He's in there. He's asleep – but I'm worried there might be a fire.' And then I realised that I was sobbing. James was sweet, he went and took a look through the window and came back in a few seconds.

'It's alright, Helen. He's still asleep, snoring his head off, but the cigarette has burned out. He's fine.'

And at that Vanessa handed me a Kleenex (I'd started crying again), announced that we should go as we'd done what we'd come to do, and we went home.

*Lord, please watch over Aaron for me, be there as he sleeps. Amen.*

## FRIDAY MAY 4th

Today I finally got to see Hayley – but I couldn't get much out of her, she just said she hated men but she hated me more. I invited Hayley to come along to the youth club tonight. She invited me to go to hell and told me that she'd rather have her head amputated. Progress is somewhat limited with Hayley. She's still angry about last Christmas.

One of the most difficult things that I have to deal with is doing difficult things to protect people who don't understand what I'm doing and resent my care. They hate me because they think I'm trying to mess up their lives, when in fact I'm trying to do the opposite. Hayley's one case in point, but I have others – I'm trying to protect these kids from parents who are inadequate, in some cases predatorial, or too out of it to care, and yet some children seem unable to get to the point where they acknowledge that their parents can do anything wrong. In fact they'd rather blame themselves than admit to the fact that their dad is bad.

Then I wondered if perhaps that happens to God all the time. There are some things that he definitely says 'No' to, that are off-limits for Christians. But that's not because God is a cosmic killjoy, who is spending eternity trying to lash up our fun, but because he knows what damage we do to ourselves when we mess around with stuff that will hurt us: he wants to save us from pain. What kind of parent would allow their child to put their hand on a hot gas cooker or in a fire, or play with rattlesnakes? Good parents say 'No.' But just as kids think that their parents are sad and don't know anything, so perhaps we do the same with God. Next time I feel resentful because as a Christian I'm not free to do whatever I want, I need to remember that the God who says 'No' does so because he is love.

Of course, that's not so easy to remember when the pressure is on . . . but *Lord, remind me.*

I'm still praying lots for Laura and Aaron. Laura is one of the funniest women I have ever met. I sort of feel bad for laughing because her humour is not the most complimentary to people, but she makes these hilarious gags while at the same time keeping her face totally straight. Sometimes I'm not even sure whether she means to be funny or not.

Today she was doing an impression of Hayley, who came screaming into the office to demand some more money. Every time she asked Laura a question, Laura replied in exactly the same voice and tone. Hayley couldn't figure out whether she was doing it on purpose or whether that was just the way she spoke. To be honest, I think she is frightened of Laura. She will eff and blind at me but she goes all quiet when Laura is around. I think she can sense that Laura won't take any of her nonsense. Plus, I'm not so sure I could take Hayley in a fight, despite being goodness knows how much older than her. Laura, on the other hand, could restrain her with one hand. Sometimes I think that the only language Hayley understands is violence. At least it's the only language she's been taught.

Nola phoned me up today and you'll never guess who turned up at her philosophy class last night? Aaron! My stomach immediately did somersaults, imagining him converting dramatically as Nola proved with logic as sharp as Jack the Ripper's knife collection that God is indeed the true Master of the Universe and that Aaron's main purpose in life is to dedicate himself to Christ. Unfortunately, he seemed obstinate and kicked up a fuss about the impossibility of the Trinity. Which to be fair, I never got either. She said that she and a few students went out for a drink afterwards and that Aaron went too and he kept going on about this girl Helen whom he respected and seemed to get the Christian thing but in a good way, despite of course faith being horribly logically flawed. Nola asked him a few more questions and she finally figured out that he was talking about me.

Apparently Nola told me about what Aaron said because she wanted to encourage me, as she knew that sometimes I didn't believe I was very good at the whole Christian thing and that I had just received some of the highest praise you can get.

'Helen, when someone who thinks that Jesus had some serious emotional issues and that Christianity is probably responsible for the death, torture and rape of half the world's population, yet believes you are a good Christian and a great person, it's time to realise you must be doing something right.'

She seemed concerned for Aaron. She mentioned that at the pub he was drinking a lot and found it difficult to concentrate on the conversation. She said that as the night wore on, he got increasingly random and she didn't think that drunkenness was the sole cause. She asked me if I could keep an eye on him, which God, as I'm sure you must know, is ironic as I'm supposed to be keeping far, far away.

I can't decide whether this is something Satan is doing to tempt me or something God is doing to look after Aaron, or even if life works like that in the first place. Maybe this is a completely random thing. I'm sure that I couldn't handle the temptation of being alone with him again. Even if he sat very quietly in the next room, the sexual tension between us means we'd still be committing some sort of lusty act. Nola said that he told her that, at night, he would try to sleep but that he was terrified of what would happen if he closed his eyes. Sometimes he couldn't tell whether he was dreaming or awake, that sometimes he would see things outside his window.

Anyway Nola invited Aaron to Dad's big meeting at the Town Hall tomorrow night and said he sounded enthusiastic about attending. I haven't seen him since that night at the café. I hope it's not horribly awkward.

*Lord, please, please, please look after Aaron. I don't think I could bear it if anything bad happened to him. Please protect him and help him get a really good night's sleep.*

Tonight, youth club was quiet but okay. One of the lads who comes seems to have some sort of Freudian nasal fixation. Honestly, it's like he's fishing for small change up there, or looking for his bike. And there's this other lad, John, who despite being clearly white and from Sussex, insists on trying to speak like a black brother from the Bronx. Unfortunately he has a slightly posh mid-Sussex accent and he keeps forgetting to be Bronx and reverts into upper class twit mode, which makes the whole thing sound utterly preposterous.

Par example, a conversation tonight:

Helen: 'Hi John, how are you?'

John: 'Hey wassup, blud?'

Helen: 'How was school today?'

John: 'Alri't, innit? Me go lookin for some hoes with me homies, miss and then me went to me mates' crib, miss and we smoke some ganja. Rather splendid ganja it was too, I must say.'

Helen: 'Lovely. How's your family?'

John: 'Well ma sista, she the hoe wot is biggin it up riding the family horse in the show jumping today and we is all hopin' she get de ribbon for first prize in the dressage. Thanks awfully for asking.'

Of course, John's not mad. He's just not figured out who he is or who he wants to be: a very common struggle among us human beings, whatever our age.

*Lord, help John come to the realisation that he is not a black rapper from New York. And help Dad tomorrow in the meeting. Let loads of people come. And may we win. Amen.*

Finally, God, some real answers to all those prayers prayed! We all bundled down to the Town Hall this afternoon for the meeting about Lawrence House. Even though we didn't have a vote or anything, my dad said that there would be a good chance we could shame them into keeping the building, whether they liked it or not. It seemed like the whole town turned up, most of them enthusiastically shaking my dad's hand, saying things like 'They won't defeat us again, you mark my words' or 'This will be our revenge for the battle of the beach huts.' My mother was in her element. She was wearing an electric blue Jackie O suit with an actual matching pillbox hat and red lipstick. She looked amazing, very sophisticated. I'd forgotten that my mother has the social networking ability of Bill Clinton on amphetamines – she had even drummed up the support of a few local celebrities. She was flitting from group to group, whispering, laughing and shooting meaningful looks at the podium.

Outside the venue, I was shocked to see Aaron with some people I'm sure I recognised from the café we went to. At first I wasn't sure because they were all wearing red and had painted their hands and faces red as well. They were all wearing gags and blindfolds and were doing some sort of drama piece which basically involved them falling over each other. I recognised Aaron because he had written 'Damn the man' on the back of his T-shirt. I wanted to go and say 'Hi' but realised that with his blindfold and gag on we weren't going to have a very productive conversation. Not that I particularly wanted to talk to him. Mostly I wanted to fling him up against the nearest wall and demand that he ravish me. I found Laura standing watching the red brigade with a bemused expression on her face, remarking wryly that she never knew painting yourself red was the answer to the world's problems and that if everybody did it, she was sure all suffering and injustice would be instantly alleviated . . .

The bad news was that the infamous Councillor Pike was chairing the meeting. Apparently, he was the same guy who presided over the beach hut affair and, at the meeting for that, had only asked the people who agreed with the project to speak. The rumour was that he had even paid some people in the audience to be on his and his cronies' side.

Anyway, eventually everybody filed in and I noticed Robert and Nola in the crowd and realised that half of the members of our church were also there. I gave them a quick wave and sat down. Nola had explained to me the night before that Mr and Mrs Hemming would not be coming because they believed that if something was the will of God, it would happen, whether we did anything or not. And that if God wanted the community to keep Lawrence House, he would find a way for it to happen without our interference, which didn't seem at all consistent with Mr Hemming's frantic and brutal evangelistic techniques, which definitely constitute interference in my book . . .

Creepy Councillor Pike opened the meeting with a greasy speech about the planned spa and waffled on about how it would only affect the community for the better, how there would be a swimming pool for the children to play in and how in this current day and age, with society's problems with obesity and bad health, that a spa was the best thing for this town to have. He went on to say that anyone who didn't agree with the sale of an otherwise empty building (that whilst standing disused was a drain on the Council's resources) didn't want the best for this community and that the income from this proposed sale would go towards fighting street crime and building new play-centres for children. It all sounded very plausible. However, halfway through his speech, my Dad stood up. Gradually the entire room swivelled round to look at him. In the end, Councillor Pike stopped speaking and looked at Dad, his mouth open. I don't think I've ever seen my father look so angry, he's usually such a self-controlled man, but right then he was shaking with rage and even I found him intimidating.

He began: 'I thank Councillor Pike for letting me speak. After the beach hut debacle, I was beginning to think that freedom of speech had all but died in Frenton. I would like to make a few things clear. Firstly, everything my colleague Councillor Pike has told you is a lie. This health spa will *not* be a place for the people of this community.'

He raised his voice slightly.

'And the reason for that, as Councillor Pike knows only too well, is that eighty per cent of the people in this community will not be able to afford to even walk through the front doors of this high-end luxury spa. Sure, children will be able to swim in the pool, as long as they are the children of the rich. This town will not be using this spa as a resource to get healthy and part of the reason for that is that most of the good people of this town are too busy spending their money on extortionate Council tax bills. That would be the same Council tax that seems to be exclusively paying for the petrol in your Porsche, Councillor Pike.'

'And now, yes, this building is standing empty and it is currently a drain on the Council's resources, so I suggest that we better make use of Lawrence House and turn it into something that the whole community can enjoy, both rich and poor alike.'

With that he sat down and the whole place started clapping and cheering. Pike looked like he was going to explode, which would have been wonderful but messy.

And then Vanessa did perhaps the craziest thing I have ever seen her do. She ran up on stage clasping something fluffy and pink to her chest, launched herself on Councillor Pike and before he could do anything to resist, had handcuffed herself to him and started yelling 'Free Lawrence House for the people' at the top of her voice. I think that everyone was supposed to join in with the chant but everyone was too stunned to say anything. Laura started giggling and I suddenly realised that the handcuffs had 'Lola's Erotic Emporium' written on them. Apparently James was in on the plot and they searched and searched for handcuffs but the only place that sold them was Lola's, a dodgy-looking place which is on one of the little side roads off the High Street. James and Vanessa had decided to make a minor moral sacrifice for the greater moral good and went out to buy them. I must admit I'd pay a lot of money to have seen that little outing.

Anyway, by now Vanessa was looking slightly shocked at what she'd done. I think that in her head it probably seemed like a great idea, but the actual reality of having a disgruntled 20 stone man latched onto your arm probably isn't that fun. He was trying to shake the cuff off, manhandling her in the process and James was standing at the side of the stage shouting that he had better not hurt her. Laura was pretty much wetting herself at all this whilst a couple of photographers (my mother's idea) were clicking away at the stage.

Councillor Pike was getting rough but there was no way out. Apparently James and Vanessa had symbolically thrown the key into the sea earlier that day, so there was no escaping the cuffs.

Suddenly Laura jumped up, mumbling something under her breath about how it's easier than you think to get out of those things, she should know because that idiot Dave had been into them. Then she jumped on stage, did something complicated with a hair clip and released Vanessa into James' waiting arms. This was a good idea, because I think if James hadn't been holding a shaken Vanessa, by the look on his face, he would probably have been punching Councillor Pike hard by now.

Anyway, the synopsis of all this is that the meeting was such a success that the Council surely can't possibly do anything but turn the building over to the community. Hurrah! Thank you God. Well done Dad. Even well done Mistress Vanessa . . .

## SUNDAY MAY 6th

Good but irritating church this morning. Robert gave an announcement thanking those who attended the meeting yesterday for their support and gave a brief report about what happened, although he didn't mention the handcuffing . . .

The irritating part came from one of the children. The Antichrist is alive and well and running round in his pants at New Wave church. He is only four and his name is Damien. To be fair, the Morrisons did think they were naming him after Saint Damien, the patron saint of leprosy, probably in a bid to cure Mr Morrison's psoriasis, which has been known to bury small children, or at least create landslides. Anyhow, after the church service, I was attempting to thank Robert for his support yesterday, when Damien Morrison, son of Satan, Antichrist on high, ran toward me, sticky fingers clenching, mouth (dripping abyss to hell) screaming, fat arms pumping, begging to be picked up. Some other children had been chasing him, probably the prophetic ones, hopefully with swords of fire, and I was obviously the first fool in his sight line who could provide him with some limited safety.

I picked him up and held him for a few seconds and he expressed his gratitude by poking me in the left eye with a podgy finger and smearing chocolate all over my new top, that I had saved up for ages to buy.

Life's like that. Good stuff and irritating stuff all mingled together.

Vanessa invited me to go to Infusion tonight where they have installed a smoke machine. I tell no lies. Halfway through the worship, which was led by a rock boy band that couldn't stop jumping about and sprinkling their adolescent dandruff on everybody at the front, they turned the machine on. It was bizarre. They had already turned out the lights and as I was being half blinded by the neon light-show, I was also being half blinded by white smoke. This took my mind totally off God and instead made me stumble about and swear slightly under my breath. Once I had regained my sight I looked around and saw that so many people seemed to either be in a state of complete ecstasy, or crying their eyes out.

I wondered whether the same thing would happen without the gimmicks and, if it does, I think we should ask the very serious question: 'Why the gimmicks?' I don't want to criticise a church that brings so many people to God every year, but it makes me feel a little uncomfortable. Why do we need all these things to worship? Jesus never had any of them and he was the most perfect Worshipper of all time. Am I turning into an Amish woman? Will I ultimately turn my back on all things modern and ride around Frenton in a horse and cart while dressed in a long Victorian gown? Who knows?

## WEDNESDAY MAY 9th

My father just phoned me crying. Crying.

I have only seen my father cry once in my life and that was when my brother Bruno fell off a horse that had the temperament of the Incredible Hulk on an off day. Bruno was knocked out by the tumble and got himself about twenty stitches in the chin in the process. My father went as white as a sheet and called an ambulance, trying to stem the flow of blood from my brother's head. After a few minutes Bruno came round, and my father breathed a huge sigh of relief and started to cry.

Then he got up and punched the horse so hard that he broke his hand. I'm sure the punch hurt Dad much more than the horse, but it was still impressive.

Anyway, Dad was crying on the phone because the Council called an emergency meeting about crime at the same time as the vote on Lawrence House was supposed to be going ahead. Crime is one of the priorities on my father's portfolio on the Council and if he hadn't attended the emergency meeting, they would have had good cause to fire him. Several other people who would have voted against Councillor Pike and his elitist health spa crew also had to attend. So, in the building committee meeting, the motion to sell Lawrence

House passed by one vote. I feel like nailing lumps of raw meat on these low-life Councillors and then setting them loose in a safari park filled with biologically mutated lions.

*Lord, it's not fair, why does greed always seem to win?*

My dad then apologised for crying on the phone and said he was embarrassed to have dumped all his sadness on me, what with me having such a stressful job . . .

. . . and then he went quiet and said that there was something very important that he wanted me to know. My dad has never left me in any doubt that he loves me; every time I see my parents I get a hug and kiss goodbye from them both and they never fail to say 'I love you.'

But perhaps, when you say it a lot, there's a danger that it can lose its impact. Anyway, when Dad said that he wanted to tell me something important, I felt a flash of nervous panic – the crisis-driven nature of my job means that I tend to think that sudden and unexpected news is probably bad.

Dad cleared his throat, coughed and said, 'Helen, I do love you very much. I wanted to make sure that you know it. You're a stunning person and a wonderful daughter. I'm so proud of you.'

It was my turn to cry now.

We talked a little bit more about bad things making us strong if we go to God with them and I gently reminded him that he's always taught me that, so now he needed to do the same thing, and I promised to pray loads for him. This battle might have been lost, I said, but the war wasn't over yet. When I put the telephone down, I wished that I felt as confident as I had sounded.

I rang Vanessa today to say that we need some serious emergency prayer. I have a list as long as my Council tax bill. First off, I need to pray for Dad and his devastation about the Council shenanigans. Then we need to pray for my up-and-coming marathon. It's getting so close and I'm scared I'll get an injury or pass out halfway through the race. My training has been going alright, though I must admit I have been missing out some days. Yesterday I was supposed to run ten miles but I didn't get out at all – felt deflated and discouraged after Dad's news. I really want to complete this marathon, if for no other reason than the cash I can raise. Stop the Traffik are doing an incredible job letting the world know about the outrage that is human trafficking. The money I raise can help – every little helps. But that makes me all the more worried that I'm not going to make it. Must be more consistent with the training.

Then there's Aaron, I still can't get him out of my head. I've actually called him a couple of times, but he's never in and doesn't own a mobile phone, as he says they poison the soul. My mother could also do with some prayer, as could Laura, Hayley and the rest of her tearaway friends. Plus there's the kids who hang out at the youth club, which is ticking along alright . . .

Anyway, I turned up at Vanessa's house and who should be sitting in the living-room but Laura herself? Apparently, after the handcuff incident at the public meeting, Laura and Vanessa got talking and had even hung out a couple of times. Of course neither of them thought to mention it to me. Theirs must be the strangest friendship in the world; even weirder then Gandhi and Saddam Hussein swapping friendship bracelets . . .

Anyway so we start praying and Laura seemed relaxed with it all, though I could only see her out of the corner of my eyes, which caused her to ask, a couple of minutes into it, whether I had a problem with my eye and did I want her to look at it?

The thing is, I was so embarrassed praying in front of her. It's not that I'm ashamed of my faith, but it was more the fact that I was ashamed of myself. I was scared of saying something that would give her a bad impression of what Christianity was like. Also, Laura sees me at work, warts and all, and I was scared she might think that all this very earnest and righteous praying was hypocritical. Vanessa seemed not to be so weird for once. Ever since she and James have started hanging out together a lot, she seems to have become more chilled out – with the obvious exception of the handcuff incident.

James, on the other hand, seems a lot weirder. The other day he walked into church with a bandanna on and announced he was taking up sky-diving.

Anyway, by the end of the prayer time, it didn't seem that we had dragged Laura through an emotional tunnel of religious abuse and she even said 'Yes' when Vanessa asked if we could pray for her. I nearly died. Vanessa put her hands on Laura's head and started praying a little too loudly but, apparently, now that they're friends, Vanessa does it a lot and Laura likes how it feels. Praise the Lord! Now I feel ashamed that I wasn't brave enough to ask Laura whether I could pray for her before. Sometimes the world needs people like Vanessa.

Then, after the prayer, we chatted a bit and Laura mentioned that one of her favourite plants in her garden seemed to be dying and whilst digging around she'd found the ground had been covered in some sort of oil and there was a cross buried at the roots. I suddenly remembered Vanessa's consecration of Laura's flower bed and stifled a giggle, though Vanessa as usual seemed impervious . . .

*Lord, thank you so much for today, prayer does seem to work. Make it work for Dad. Amen.*

## THURSDAY MAY 24th

It's been a whole two weeks and not much has happened, hence my lax journalling habits. No further developments on Lawrence House, although it doesn't seem like the sale to the spa company has gone through yet. Perhaps the nasty lawyers who work for the nasty Councillors are doing the paperwork behind the scenes. Marathon training going well – been following my training schedule without a hitch. Great. Bible reading not going so well.

Vanessa said the sweetest thing to me today. She burst through my front door and announced 'Helen, I'm getting married.' This was news to me because I didn't even know Vanessa fancied anyone.

'Does he know about it? I said, as a sort of joke.

'Nope', she replied, 'he hasn't even asked me out yet, but I'm sure it's going to happen. I've been praying a lot about it and I feel like it's the right thing.'

'Well, who is it?' I pressed, an inkling of suspicion already rising in my mind.

'James, of course, who else?'

Before she said it, I never would have thought of those two together, but it makes perfect sense. He always seems to be a bit more animated around her and she always seems to be a bit more mentally stable when he's in tow. Vanessa wouldn't think he was boring, because Vanessa doesn't find anything boring. It's all part of her personality – she thinks that everything is amazingly interesting, fascinating and either sent by God or the devil to test, strengthen or give us some sort of celestial message.

*Lord, please let James fall desperately in love with Vanessa and let them live their lives happily ever after. Please don't let either of them get hurt.*

## SATURDAY JUNE 30th

I haven't written this journal for over a month – horrors! Lots of reasons . . . the pace of life, training, youth club, work, etc etc being the main ones . . . Marathon training well on track, but increasingly time-consuming.

Read Psalm 14, which says that to say there is no God is the work of the fool. Thought about Aaron and prayed that he would be delivered from his folly and then remembered that he had said that he still believed in God, but couldn't figure the whole Christian thing out. Haven't seen or heard from Aaron since the red brigade incident at the public meeting . . .

Vanessa has now declared her undying love for James and apparently he's desperately in love with her too, which is helpful. He even produced a poem from his pocket that he had been working on all week to give to her, which Vanessa has learnt off by heart and stapled to her bra. Praise be to God. I can see another one of those quickie engagements coming that Christians like to pull off so much.

Of course, it does make me feel slightly bad that I'm still single. Okay, who am I kidding, it makes me feel like the spinster hag of lonely land. But I'm still happy for them. Praise the Lord indeed.

## SATURDAY JULY 14th

Yikes. Another two weeks of journal silence. Youth club fine, Hayley the same, Vanessa and James in bliss, Laura lunching with Vanessa weekly, church good, Hemmings quiet, running great. Silence from Aaron still.

I am now existing on a diet of chocolate-flavoured whey and protein bars. I have decided that a French fry will never pass my lips again for the rest of my days and have almost decided to seriously limit my alcohol intake.

I went to the gym today. Why is it that actually going to the gym is harder than working out? It's as if my body screams blood-curdling protests at the thought of weight training. Mrs Hemming was there again in her gigantic passion killer gym gear. Glad to see that she is doing her bit to prevent the male of the species drifting into wanton lust . . .

I am desperately trying to prevent myself from becoming a health bore. Just a few months ago I was happily munching my way through a mountain of biscuits every day and my preference for a happy death would have involved drowning in a chocolate-filled trough. And yet now I find myself not only checking my calorie consumption and body fat index, but I also have an urgent need to give everybody I meet an update of (a) how many pounds I have lost (b) what my resting heart rate is (c) how many miles I have run today and (d) how many of my clothes I need to throw away because of my newly discovered svelte hour-glass figure (I exaggerate slightly). Not only that, but I also want to snatch their burgers out of their hand. How swiftly the chomper becomes the self-righteous teacher of others . . .

## SUNDAY AUGUST 19th
## MARATHON DAY!

And yet another month when my diary has been neglected. Why is it that I get one part of my life in order, only to discover that other areas goes into havoc mode? Finished reading through the Psalms and am now into reading Nehemiah, which is nice and would be of special interest to those who work in the construction industry.

After all of the disappointment with the loss of Lawrence House (still no developments yet, but the silence is ominous and Dad doesn't mention it any more) today has been like a rainbow that suddenly appears like magic after a downpour.

After preparing for this day for months, I finally got to run the marathon today. Call me an endorphin junkie if you like, but I am tapping this journal entry into my computer in the car on the way home. This was a one-off and I must record my elated feelings so that I can enjoy them again later and before I start to forget – again, the benefits of journalling. Need a clear mind to recount all the events of the day. Not easy with the computer balanced on my knees but I'll do my best.

Woke up and bounced out of bed, eager to get on with the challenge ahead. The sun was shining for once and I worried that it might be too hot to run in. Mum and Dad phoned last night to wish me well, which was lovely. I then began the day with a hearty breakfast of eggs, bacon, fried bread and mushrooms – obviously absolutely nothing healthy about this whatsoever but decided that as I'm going to expend about a zillion calories by hurtling my body along a 26.2 mile course, then I need all of the proteins, fat, carbohydrates and whatever else is secreted in a British fry-up.

I packed my sports bag and then James and Vanessa came and picked me up. James said he wanted to be there to provide support and Vanessa will be praying for me every step of the way, she says. Headed to the start, but had to abandon the car eventually and walk. When we got there, I felt immediately intimidated with the same feeling that I got at the start of Together for the Kingdom. The place was teeming with marathoners. Admittedly, not all of them looked like accomplished athletes and there were one or two who looked as if they wouldn't survive the first two hundred yards, but there were enough finely honed athletic types to make me feel like a Robin Reliant driver at a Formula 1 race meeting.

The major blow of the day was that Kristian was also there – as a runner. He'd certainly kept that quiet. We've haven't spoken much since the infamous incident in the chalet, but there he was, all irritating and stud-like in his big bingalong Australian shorts, more suitable for surfing than running but undeniably trendy, and wearing an oversized T-shirt with a graffiti design. He didn't even have proper running shoes, but was obviously planning to make a fashion statement as he wore his Vans. He may walk with a limp for the rest of his life, but he'll look good as he staggers. His beaming girlfriend was there too, obviously his appointed cheerleader for the day. She shot me another one of those 'Greetings, O freak' looks. I decided to smile and wave but confess that I was grinding my teeth together as I did it. He smiled at me as if we were the best of friends. 'Good luck, Hel', he said, giving me the impression that he thought that I was definitely going to need it. What makes it even more irritating is that I actually saw him – there were so many people there that I am sure if I had wanted to spot him, I wouldn't have been able to.

I drenched myself in water and then the starter's gun went off. All the runners are given numbers that reflect how fast they think they are going to complete the course, which means all the really serious ones go off first, and the rest of us come along behind, in order of our capabilities – or inflated hopes, in Kristian's case. He must have thought he was going to be as good as me, though as far as I know he has done absolutely no training – I've never seen him out running. It means that you start the marathon walking because of the crush of people, and it was a good mile before the crowd had thinned out enough for me to be able to start actually running – I had visions of walking the whole course, which was daft . . .

The first couple of miles were very hard, simply because my brain kept telling me that I had so long to go. I've found that the brain is the biggest challenge with running. One training manual actually suggests trying to fool your brain when you get up in the morning by telling yourself that you're not going to run. You're supposed to change into your running gear, while all the while telling yourself, 'I'm not going to run today.' You grab some coffee and then when your brain isn't noticing, you make a dash for the door and make a run for it – literally. But about three miles in, I had a wonderful surprise – Laura appeared behind a crash barrier, screaming 'Go Helen! Go Helen!' I had no idea she was coming. She even ran alongside me for a few yards, and I panted out how lovely it was of her to come. 'Nonsense' she said. 'We all need someone to yell for us . . . '

At mile 5 my brain was screaming at me to lie down on the pavement, order a pizza and take a nap, so I practised my little positive thinking tricks to keep me going through to mile 6 and beyond. I thought of words like 'power' and 'glide' and 'winner.' Not sure if this is slightly New Agey but it seems to work. It was as I started on mile 7 that I got what I'm ashamed to say was a delicious surprise, that I enjoyed far more than I should have.

I got around a long bend and saw Kristian at the side of the road, bent over and throwing up. His girlfriend was nowhere to be seen, still back near the starting line, but there were enough people in the crowd watching for this to be embarrassing for Kristian. He was now treating about four hundred people to a public display of vomiting – not exactly the profile and platform that he would have chosen.

I'd seen Kristian shoot off like a hare on fire as soon as the crush had thinned enough to let him, but now he was in a right state. He hobbled onto the pavement, lay down and groaned – obviously those Vans had not served him well. Did I gloat? As if . . .

Kristian even gasped out 'I think I might have flu . . . ' as I cantered by. Oh per – lees! Thought about stopping but he had the St John's Ambulance people with him and starting again is so hard . . . and the temptation to have said something might have proved too much for me.

As I jogged away, I suddenly realised why it is that I so dislike Kristian. He can't admit his weaknesses. He's out of the race, not because of some mystery bug but because he probably didn't train, is arrogant enough to think he can do anything and was more concerned about looking cool than wearing the right gear. But he can't face all of that, so he has to pretend that he's been mugged by a germ. Pathetic.

I carried on and then was totally stunned at mile 14 to hear Vanessa's voice booming at me. 'COME ON, HELEN SLOANE! VICTORY'S IN SIGHT. DON'T BACK OFF NOW. YOU AND GOD CAN DO IT!'

Vanessa and James and Laura had met up (they were in on the secret of her coming) and had walked to the 14 mile point – the course doubles back on itself so they had to go a much shorter distance than me! – and waited there for me. It's probably psychological, but it was as if fresh power surged into my legs as I heard them clapping and cheering.

Prayed for death at mile 21, which was where I hit the infamous wall. The wall is where you feel that you have absolutely no physical or emotional resources left – you want to give up. Carrying on was simply a matter of cold choice – no feelings, no emotions, nothing but 'I'm going to do this.' Managed to get through that terrible phase and at last saw the finish line in sight. Once again, I could hear Vanessa's voice bellowing out at me. She was actually yelling that bit from the Bible about running the race to win, at the top of her voice. Laura and James were clapping and cheering and at last, feeling like a corpse, I crossed the line.

Which is when I experienced a resurrection of sorts. Suddenly, my near dead body and dull mind seemed to register that I had done it – I'd finished the course, I'd raised the money, I was a marathoner. I allowed Laura and James to hug me and Vanessa did one of her little charismatic dances, which no-one seemed to notice.

It was wonderful. I must call Mum and Dad to tell them about my massive sporting breakthrough. I'm looking forward to a long hot bath. Oh, my mobile's battery is gone, and the computer's going the same way . . . will finish this diary la . . .

## TUESDAY AUGUST 21st

Nothing.

## WEDNESDAY AUGUST 22nd

Nothing to say.

## FRIDAY AUGUST 24th

Numb.

## MONDAY AUGUST 27th

Numb.

I don't know where to start. I've got to try to get my thoughts down somewhere. Feel so numb, so dead.

I can't bring myself to write it down here though. The front page of the Frenton Gazette says it all. I can't even bear to read it again.

# LOCAL COUNCILLOR MURDERED: POLICE APPEAL FOR WITNESSES

Wellknown local Councillor Peter Sloane (67) was fatally stabbed last Saturday evening in what police describe as a 'senseless and brutal attack'. It took place outside the King's Head pub on Frenton High Street around 11.30pm.

In a statement issued earlier today, a police spokesman said that passersby became alarmed when a large gang of youths, some of whom were obviously drunk, started goading a young man who was walking past the pub. They then attacked the young man, who cannot be named for legal reasons. Mr. Sloane was driving past, saw the fracas and stopped to intervene.

Police say that according to witnesses' reports, the gang then turned on Mr. Sloane, kicking and punching him, before repeatedly stabbing his chest and arms. The police and ambulance services were called, but Mr. Sloane died at the scene.

Mr. Sloane became a well-known figure in Frenton after his unsuccessful campaign against beach hut developments last year. Insisting that Frenton-on-Sea Borough Council conduct themselves with greater openness and accountability, Mr. Sloane was, in recent weeks, an outspoken opponent of the plans to develop Lawrence House into a private health spa. He delivered a speech at the recent public enquiry and gathered considerable local support, but the Buildings Committee of the Council subsequently met and voted in favour of the spa development.

Councillor Aubrey Pike, leader of the Council, offered this tribute today:

'Peter Sloane will be sadly missed by myself and all members of the Council, whatever their political affiliation. He and I did not always see eye to eye, but he was a worthy opponent. We are all horrified at this terrible, outrageous crime and appeal to anyone who may be able to assist the police with their enquiries to step forward immediately. Finally, we would like to say that this is even more tragic because our crime rates are so low in Frenton. Future visitors and tourists may come here knowing that a warm, safe welcome awaits them.'

Police request that any witnesses should contact them immediately on 02243 777777 and assure the public that all responses will be treated in confidence.

Laura and Vanessa are encouraging me to write this, but I don't know why. I've got nothing to pray and nothing to say. He's dead. He's dead. My wonderful mother got the news the night it happened, but decided not to tell me until I had done the marathon. 'Your dad would have wanted you to run that race' she said 'because of all the training you had done and the money you were raising.' So it wasn't until I borrowed James's mobile on the way home to tell my parents about my run – and completing the marathon in less than five hours – that Mum could blurt out the terrible news.

James took me to the house right away, but the police were there. Mum kept breaking down while she talked to them and I sat there and held her hand. Apparently the gang fled and no-one has stepped forward to offer any leads or point to any suspects, although the police are still doing forensics with the knife. They stabbed him thirteen times. Thirteen. And whoever did this was either drunk, or drugged up, or mad, or all three. They slashed him so terribly. Neither Mum or I could bear going to the mortuary to identify him and Bruno is still in between ports and is going to get the first flight home when he arrives in Ocho Rios and so James was kind enough to do the identification for us. Faithful James.

One of the worst things about death is the fact that life goes on as if everything is still the same. I had to get some shopping in today and as I wandered around the stores throwing supplies into my trolley, I noticed that other people were going about their lives as if nothing had happened. I wanted to stop and shake them, let them know that my dad is dead. The trouble is, they know. They've read the papers and murders don't happen here often – this is the talk of the town, but still they go shopping and rent DVDs and life moves on and I have to go shopping too.

My life has to keep going. Just when I thought things couldn't get any worse, I had to go and see Hayley today. I got a couple of days off for compassionate leave, but the funeral has been delayed because of forensics and the post-mortem report is still pending and I was going mad anyway, so I went back to work.

I went to Hayley's house.

'I heard about your dad', she said, matter of factly.

For a moment, I thought that she was going to say something kind, something comforting – that would have been the obvious thing.

'So now you know how it feels, miss. You took my dad away from me. Now you've lost yours. How do you like it, eh?'

I wanted to wipe that grinning, evil sneer off her face and perhaps that's what she was looking for – a slap that would have cost me my job and then I'd have lost my career as well as my father. I couldn't speak, she stunned me into silence.

Thank God for friends. Vanessa has been fantastic, all prayers and notes and phone calls. James has been wonderful too – in fact everybody, people from the church like Robert and Nola and others – they've all been great. I even got a gift from Aaron. It was a Christian CD out of his old collection that he'd never got round to throwing away, and a note to say that I was in his thoughts.

Even Mr and Mrs Hemming sent a sympathy card.

Enough. Must sleep now.

Bruno flew in from South America this morning. It's weird, when we were younger we were inseparable, but these days we hardly speak. I'm not sure how he's going to take this. He hasn't been around for the last few years and he's always been travelling in some far-off country. He was rebellious as a teenager and him and Dad never saw eye-to-eye. I'm sure he feels terrible that he wasn't here when it happened. I don't know whether he and Dad spoke much in the last couple of years, although I know Dad sent him a lot of emails. Occasionally we got a postcard from him from Thailand or a cracked phone call from Egypt, usually asking if we could lend him some money. Thinking about it, he owes me £300. I've always been the sensible one and he's been the free spirit, always up for an adventure, with a gift of the gab that serves him well with the ladies. As teenagers they were always falling in love with him, but he never seemed to notice too much.

The last I heard he was with some Australian girl called Angie who has red hair down to her waist. I hadn't even realised he was in South America. I thought he was still being a beach bum in Australia somewhere. I used to have these panic attacks that he would get stung by a box-jellyfish or eaten by a shark or something. I haven't even spoken to him properly yet. The minute he got home he went straight to his room, shut the door and now appears to be asleep. It must have been a long journey home.

I hate. It's ironic really. I hate because I loved. I can't stop thinking about those teenagers who did that to my father.

*Lord, I know I'm supposed to forgive and I can say it as much as you want but I don't mean it. My lips are willing but my heart is numb.*

James and Vanessa and Katy have taken over the running of the youth club. To think, one of those kids might have even been there, might have even joined in, they might even know who did it. I want to beat them all senseless until they tell me the truth. I want justice. No, I don't. I want to hurt the scum who did this to my dad.

What do you wear to a funeral? What do you wear to your father's funeral? I hadn't even thought of it until now and I have to leave in half an hour. I tried on my black dress and then realised that my black dress made my cleavage look more 'Come and get me boys' than 'My father has been stabbed to death by a gang of unidentified youths on whom I wish to perpetrate vigilante violence.' Do you even have to wear black to funerals these days? Will people think I don't love my father enough if I don't wear black? Am I allowed to wear make-up? Blow dry my hair?

I have rung my mother. She is wearing her electric blue Jackie O suit. She said it was one of my Dad's favourite things – he loved her wearing it. I have decided on black trousers, white shirt with purple cardigan and flat shoes.

So I survived yesterday's funeral. Where do I start? How do I feel? That's a difficult question to answer. I knew people died everyday, in horrible unfair ways but when it happens to someone close to you, you realise what a dark place this world truly is. My Father is dead and nothing can change that. Death doesn't belong here. That's why it hurts us so much.

Have you ever cried so hard that you start sounding inhuman? Perhaps one day I'll stop crying myself to sleep every night, perhaps one day it will get better. Perhaps I will stop having all the other odd things that I'm told are part of grief but which feel like I'm going mad . . . like hearing Dad in the next room, or thinking I saw him catching a bus last week – he never caught buses, for goodness' sake – or feeling sick or shouting at the television or having a huge email argument with a colleague and copying in the entire office by accident or . . . And if anyone else asks me whether I am through the first stage of grief yet, I shall hit them. There are no stages – just a series of states, each one worst than the last . . . anger, guilt (why wasn't I there to protect him?) . . . the 'If onlys' . . . and the pain. I never knew that grief could actually be a physical pain, and painkillers don't touch it. Alcohol numbs it but then I feel worse the next day.

I didn't realise how many people would turn up to the funeral. It was held at the little church my parents went to in the village and there were even people crammed in the vestry. Everybody from my church was there and although I secretly wished that's where it could have been held, my mother insisted that it be at the parish church. She said it was the place Dad chose to worship, so that's where we should choose to honour him. The vicar seemed nice in a distant, bumbling sort of way but before the funeral he visited my parents' cottage and asked us if we would like to choose any particular hymns or readings. We chose Psalm 91, Isaiah 40:21-31, and John 14, all about the mansions etc . . . and some of Dad's favourite hymns.

Going through all the things that have been written about grief made me realise that not only do people suffer this terrible thing every day, but also that they survive it too. People have survived the most horrific things, I don't know how, but they do and this gives me hope. If only this terrible heartache would stop.

I am finding it so difficult to pray. I don't think I blame God for what happened, but at the same time I have nothing to say to him. Right after my mother told me about it, I prayed that God would raise Dad from the dead, and of course he didn't. Since then I don't have anything to say. I'd like God to stop me feeling so terrible, but then I also think that would be disrespectful to my father. I loved him so much, it should feel this terrible. During the funeral his coffin was displayed at the front and I couldn't stop imagining him lying in there. Then I looked around at the church that was supposed to be about life and resurrection and yet there was this dead man in it, my lovely kind smiling dead dad, and he couldn't be woken.

I wanted him to sit up and tell me that I'd had enough pain to make me strong, so now he'd decided to come back to us all. During the service we sang *Abide with me,* and I was struck by the words:

> I need Thy presence every passing hour.
> What but Thy grace can foil the tempter's power?
> Who, like Thyself, my guide and stay can be?
> Through cloud and sunshine,
> Lord, abide with me . . .

I realised that the one prayer I could pray, one that I could mean, was this simple. *Jesus, stay close. Even though it feels like you're a billion miles away.*

After the hymn my mother went to the front and spoke about my father a little bit. She told everybody how they had met in a library whilst he was at university and she pretended to be a student too so he wouldn't think she was stupid. She was actually working at the local pub at the time. Then she said that she had been turning to God through this time of tragedy and how much Jesus was helping her through. Bizarrely, this gave me mixed feelings. I was so glad my mother was finding some love and support somewhere, but I felt slightly cheated. I was the one who had been a Christian all these years and yet it was my mother who seemed to be getting all the comfort from God. I have never felt as far away from God as I do now, but my mother has apparently never felt closer.

Anyway, a couple of other things happened at the funeral, one that made me want to literally cheer and one that threw me into total confusion. Firstly, the Hemmings have finally left New Wave Christian Fellowship. Perhaps it's unkind of me to be happy about that, but frankly my father has been stabbed to death and I'll search for any kind of happiness I can get. When they first turned up to the funeral I was annoyed, but there were so many other people there and so many things to do that I didn't think any more about them. Even Councillor Pike was there. I managed to shoot him some looks which were so dirty that I'm surprised they didn't strike him dead.

After the funeral everyone had gone into a room at the back of the church and were nervously picking at the food my mother and I had prepared, everyone apart from the vicar who was wolfing down half a plate of cucumber sandwiches that he later congratulated my mother on. I don't think the poor man knew what else to say. In fact, this seems to be a running theme at funerals. I suppose it's because there's nothing much you can say, that saying you're sorry doesn't and can't cover all the bases. It's weird to watch people dealing with death in different ways. Some nervously try to avoid your gaze because they know that they can't bring anyone back to life and therefore can't make it better and some babble on about the traffic and, well, the cucumber sandwiches. I hate cucumber sandwiches.

My mother was talking to Robert and Nola when suddenly Mr and Mrs Hemming bustled up to them. It was then I got a horrible feeling in my stomach, a stomach that was already feeling queasy, so I moved closer. I heard Mr Hemming tell my mother that it had been an 'interesting' funeral. Then Mrs Hemming moved in, in a conspiratorial way.

'You know, Kitty, is it? It's hard to lose a loved one, but we must remember that God is sovereign and if he chooses to take someone away, we must accept that it is his will and get on with things.'

My mother gave her a look. I know that look. It's a warning. Carry on at your peril. I've seen it on my mother's face before – only once or twice, but I'd recognise it anywhere.

'Yes, Kitty', Mr Hemming added. 'The Lord decided that your husband should suffer this fate, for one reason or another. He is in charge. We thank him even though we don't understand, convinced that ultimately his will has been done.'

With this my mother drew back her hand and slapped Mr Hemming's face so hard that he actually rocked on his feet and had to clutch onto Mrs Hemming for support. He yelled and then turned to Robert, who had moved in closer, sensing trouble at the same time as I did.

Mr Hemming almost shouted at Robert. 'I think we need to pray for this woman, she is obviously mad with grief.' Robert stared at Mr Hemming, his nostrils flared with anger. He said nothing.

'Robert!' Mrs Hemming barked, 'Answer my husband! He is a deacon in your church and he's just been assaulted!'

Robert carried on staring at him and I noticed he was breathing heavily. Nola had by now put her hand on his arm and was looking worried.

At last Robert spoke, softly and slowly. 'No', he said and paused. And then he turned to my mum.

'Kitty, I am so sorry for what has happened here.'

'Rebuke that woman!' screamed Mrs Hemming. 'We demand you rebuke that woman!' Mr Hemming was going redder and redder in the face. Then he drew himself up stiffly and announced 'My wife is right. If you do not rebuke that woman, then I'll . . . I'll . . . I'll resign!'

Robert said nothing. The silence grew and grew.

And that was that. They both stomped out without another word. And they have resigned from the church. Robert says they are still welcome, but only if they refrain from handing out any of their unChristlike advice. My mother said that she felt much better after hitting someone and that she wished Mr Hemming would come back and say something else stupid so that she could slap him again.

Nola laughed and said that if Mum hadn't slapped him, Robert probably would have and then he would have been the one losing his position, not Mr Hemming. To be honest, I was relieved by all the drama. For a while there had been something else to focus on, apart from my father's death and that made me feel happy, wondering whether I wouldn't have to go through life thinking about how much I missed him, every second of the day.

And so to the second thing that happened at the funeral. The second thing is a secret for now, a complicated, screwed-up secret that I wish I didn't know but, confusingly, I'm glad that I do. Maybe glad isn't the right word. I'd prefer to know it rather than not know it, but at the same time I wish that I *didn't* know it and didn't have to make that kind of decision.

I had gone outside the church for some fresh air when I noticed a figure half-hiding behind a tree. I peered at it, wondering who it was, and I realised it was Aaron. He looked a mess. He had a black eye – actually more like a black eye, black cheek and black lip. He appeared to have been crying. A lot.

In fact, he looked like he had been crying more than I had, which was impressive as I thought I had been setting a new world record. I'm sure he was also drunk; in fact I was certain he was drunk unless he happened to have mugged a homeless alcoholic for his clothes. In fact, he looked like he had mugged a homeless alcoholic for his clothes and then gone out and got drunk.

'What's the matter?' I asked. Despite the actual fact that it was I who was at my father's funeral and so therefore I was the one who should have been getting some sympathy . . .

'I'm sorry', he blurted out. 'I'm really so sorry . . . '

'You look more upset than I do', I replied. 'You almost look like it was your dad who died.' With this, he bent over double and groaned, as though I'd hit him hard in the stomach.

'For goodness sake, Aaron. I really don't want to hear about your problems right now. There is a room full of people in there, who are all trying to be nice to me. And in a minute I've got to pretend that I can hold a normal conversation without wanting to cry so hard I stop breathing and you're out here, drunk and being crazy, as usual. I don't think I can deal with you right now.'

He looked up at me, his eyes swollen red and slurred 'Helen, look, I need to tell you something. I don't think I'm supposed to because of the police investigation and everything, but I thought you should know . . . '

'Police investigation? What police investigation?' For the moment I thought that he'd been arrested for drugs or something and now was showing up here to whine to me about his stupidity . . .

'Helen. It was me. I was the guy those kids were attacking when your father stopped his car. I managed to get away as he was talking to them, I thought he'd be okay. I thought he could just get into his car and drive away if they got violent. So I ran into the pub to call the police. When I got back, they had gone and your dad was lying there, lying there like a doll or something. At first I didn't even think he was real. He was unconscious, losing so much blood. I held him, Helen, I want you to know that. He didn't die by himself. I should have stayed. I should have protected him. I'm so sorry. But I did hold him and his blood soaked into my clothes and got into my hair and I held him and I didn't let go. Not till a long time after he was gone, just in case. I know that changes nothing, Helen, but it's the only thing I have.'

And that was that. He stared at me for a while, eyes wide, pleading, then stumbled away. I tried to call after him but he didn't seem to hear. I didn't even know what I was going to say. Part of me feels so sorry for him. But part of me, part of me thinks, I would prefer for him to be dead right now, if that meant that my father would still be alive. If I could swap their lives, I'd do it in a blink of an eye. I'd do it right now.

## FRIDAY SEPTEMBER 21st

It's been a week since the funeral and nothing much has changed. I decided not to try to track Aaron down. Later, maybe. Who knows? This week's newspaper reports an interesting story:

# NATIONAL CAMPAIGN TO STOP LUXURY SPA GROWS

Tension is rising this week in Frenton-on-Sea Borough Council as the national media increases pressure on party leader, David Howard, over the Peter Sloane murder. Sloane, a local Councillor in Frenton, was campaigning over the sale of Lawrence House, a Council-owned building.

Questions have arisen over the intended sale of the building and a source who asked not to be identified has confirmed that the wife of the Councillor behind the decision, Councillor Aubrey Pike, 56, is the sister-in-law of James Burton, 45, the businessman who intended to purchase the property. Burton is a property magnate whose chain of exclusive health spas can be found in almost every major city in the country.

Peter Sloane's untimely and tragic death has not only become the source of national media attention, but has also prompted further protests over the planned sale of Lawrence House. Media focus and a public letter-writing campaign have bombarded the Council with demands that the building be dedicated to the memory of Sloane and turned into a community centre. Last month local hero Sloane was brutally kicked and stabbed to death outside the King's Head pub. He was intervening in the attack of another man who escaped with minor injuries. A family man, Sloane leaves wife Kitty (56) daughter Helen (27) and son Bruno (25).

The Council has invited me to move the youth club to Lawrence House. Apparently they have finally caved in to public opinion and want to dedicate the whole building to the local community, with services for all ages, babies, children, youth – all through to the old. It would mean much better facilities, everything we wanted, really . . .

. . . and I couldn't care less. I'm the last person who should be allowed to look after young people. For goodness sake, I have violent fantasies about what I would do to them (well a certain group of them) if I ever tracked them down.

Though it is getting a little better. I saw Hayley yesterday and I didn't hate her as much as usual, but if my feelings don't change significantly, I'm going to have to give up my job. And that's ironic, because being a social worker and working with young people is the only thing I ever wanted to do. I may despise Hayley, but I don't know whether I could entrust her to someone else's care. I know so much about her life now, though I wish I knew more. What if they didn't do their job properly? What would happen to her? What will happen to her anyway?

I phoned my mother and asked her if I should do it. She thought for a long time and said, 'Darling, I don't know, your father was always the one to give out advice for decisions like this. I suppose if you can't do it, then you shouldn't. But at the same time, I know this is what you wanted, before all of this, before this terrible thing happened to us. I'm not sure. Try to think about what your father would say.'

Then I phoned Nola and asked if she could pray for me. These days I seem to find it difficult to pray for myself. It's like one of those dreams where you're trying to say something, but try as you might, nothing comes out of your mouth. You try to scream but you find your throat has closed over and you've lost your voice. The silence is deafening.

Nola's coming round tomorrow.

## FRIDAY SEPTEMBER 28th

Nola came round and prayed for me. I feel a little better. I think I am finding it hard to pray because I'm still so angry inside, not just at God, but at the whole world, at whoever it was who murdered my father and at everybody else for not protecting him. Also, if I pray I have to think about all those questions about suffering and I don't have the energy for it all. As Nola prayed for me today, I felt a little bit of that anger and weariness shift. It was like a glimmer of hope appeared from somewhere, but I don't know whether I'll ever get rid of this rage and for some reason I don't know whether I even want to – even though it's so exhausting. Anyway, I've made a surprising decision – at least I was surprised by my own choice. I have decided to go ahead with the youth club move. I didn't have a big miraculous experience or anything, but I've decided that I think that's what my dad would have wanted. The whole community centre is part of the legacy that he has left and who better to be involved than his own daughter? I'm not sure how it will go but I've asked James, Vanessa, Nola and Robert to pray for me lots. *Lord, please let their prayers make a real difference, because I can't pray much any more.*

I'm not any better but I'm too tired to feel anything much. Working so hard means I collapse into bed exhausted at night and I don't have to dwell on what happened to Dad. There are all sorts of admin things to do in order to get ready to move the youth club to its new venue, even though it isn't ready yet and won't be for some time. I hate paperwork . . .

We are going to have a memorial service for Dad in a week or so. It was Councillor Pike's idea. I still don't find him easy to like, but he came to Mum, and said he thought it would be a wonderful way of celebrating Dad's life. All the Councillors are coming – those he fought with and those he fought alongside. I guess it is Pike's way of saying he is sorry. It means more planning, more ideas.

The Memorial Service was quite an event. As I sit on my bed now, writing this, I feel okay. Sort of. The pain of my father's death is still like a stab in my heart. But I'm happier, I think, in a different, more complicated type of happiness than I'm used to, but happier nonetheless.

We held the service in the church, because it could accommodate all the people, and asked Robert to do a short talk at the end, explaining a little bit about my father's faith. I believe that my father's death was totally meaningless and unplanned – but if God can use it in the slightest way for good, than I want him to. God wasn't the architect of his death – but he can be the redeemer of it. My father used his life for good and I think he would have wanted his death used for good as well. And lots of Councillors, and people he had worked with, and neighbours and friends – they all wanted to be able to say something about what Dad had meant to them. We had to limit them in the end, or the service would have gone on for hours.

It seemed like half the town showed up. Aaron came too. I noticed him standing at the back. All the Councillors, everybody. It was horribly sad and yet comforting at the same time – how can something be so bittersweet?

Robert spoke with the warmth and kindness that makes us all love him so much.

'Peter Sloane was a good man, but Peter Sloane was also a Christian man. Sadly, those are two statements that don't necessarily go hand in hand. But Peter understood what it was to be a true Christian, to be the kind of person that Jesus was. Peter was a man who hated corruption and loved his community. Like Jesus, Peter's vision was to try to look after those who have nowhere else to go and to care about those who don't have the opportunities that many others enjoy. So he would have been overjoyed that Lawrence House will, in time, become the Peter Sloane Community Centre – dedicated to the people he cared about. People mattered to him: it is no exaggeration to say Peter literally gave up his life so that another person might live. He went to the aid of a young man under attack and it cost Peter his life.'

'If there is a prayer in your heart for Christ or for the new Community centre, then I'd like to invite you, as a symbol of that prayer, to come up here and light a candle and place it on the table behind me.'

Almost at once people started coming forward. I think Robert and Nola must have used up Ikea's entire supply of night lights. After lighting mine, I was about to walk forward, when I turned and caught Aaron's eye. He had moved to stand a little closer to me and now he was shyly picking his way to the front. He looked up and as he saw me, he looked worried and wavered, as if he was going to turn back. By now his bruises had faded and he was back in his usual garb of black polo neck and skinny jeans. He looked tired. I smiled at him and nodded, as if to say, go on, it's alright, go ahead. He nodded nervously back.

Suddenly, someone flicked a switch and turned the lights off and once again me and Aaron found ourselves staring at each other in the candle light, just like we did in the poetry café, a lifetime ago. Strangely, I don't think that either of us wanted to be the first one to look away. I remembered how we had spun around those lamp posts, how everything was so much easier back then, even though I didn't realise it. I wanted to be on that sofa again with him, without any other thought in the world. And yet because of him my father was dead.

He made his way up to the table and placed his lit candle on it, came back down again and slipped into the back of the crowd. I watched him go, feeling confused, knowing it might be a very long time before I could speak to him again. And then I walked slowly towards the table, flickering candle in hand.

I couldn't hold back the tears as I looked at the dozens of flickering candles that covered the table. I placed my down and whispered 'Thanks, lovely Dad. I miss you and I hate it that you're not here. But if God will stick with me, I think I could be strong.'

I dabbed my eyes with a tissue and went back to sit back down again. And it was then that I noticed Laura was sitting a couple of seats down from me with her eyes closed. She must have sensed someone looking at her – as she opened her eyes and looked at me.

'Just thought I'd try praying how Vanessa prays,' she said, 'though without being completely mental, of course.'

I suddenly got the giggles, remembering Vanessa stalking round Laura's garden, burying crosses and killing her plants with communion wine.

'What?' Laura asked, giggling herself now. 'What's so funny?'

'Nothing', I replied, 'just thinking about Vanessa and her craziness. I like it sometimes, to be honest.'

'Me too' said Laura. 'I've never known anyone so passionate about God and all that Christian stuff before. We all know she's a bit barmy and yet there's something solid there, buried deep in her somewhere, and whenever I'm with her, you know, I feel completely safe. Like she loves me and I don't know why, but that makes me want to pray.'

'I know exactly what you mean', I replied.

And then suddenly, someone somewhere flicked the lights back on and I got the shock of my life. Hayley had come. She was leaning against a pillar, wearing a tracksuit and gold earrings so big you could have used them for hoopla. Her hair was scraped so far back off her temples she looked like she'd had an over-enthusiastic facelift. She looked up, caught my eye and gave me the usual scowl, before returning her glare to the floor. I couldn't believe it. She shows up at my father's memorial service and she's still the same sulky adolescent mess.

Then she turned and looked across at me for a second and then looked down immediately, awkward and uncomfortable, which is no wonder, considering all her hideous jibes.

I felt like walking right over there and kicking her out. I wasn't going to allow her to ruin this.

But then, after looking down for a second or two, her head came up again and her eyes met mine. I decided to try.

I waved and nodded a hello, still expecting that she might return the compliment with a two-fingered signal or a sneer. But she raised her hand, waved back and mouthed 'Hi Helen . . . '

And it was then that I saw it, on Hayley's face. It was so fleeting I could have missed it. But I saw it.

It was the slightest hint, like sunshine peering for a second from behind a cloud, of a smile.

Helen's marathon run was to support STOP THE TRAFFIK, which continues to campaign against the horrific trade that is human trafficking. Please visit www.stopthetraffik.org and add your voice to the millions around the world who insist that trafficking must stop. And please support STOP THE TRAFFIK financially. Visit the web site and donate there – you can give online, by text, or by shopping online.

For news of Jeff Lucas's ministry, to access his blog, or to purchase resources, visit **www. jefflucas.org**